CW01636855

CHRISTMAS IN BRANDEN BAY

KELLY MASON

LITTLE ORCHARD PRESS

Copyright © 2022 by Kelly Mason

All rights reserved.

No part of this book may be reproduced in any form or by any electronic or mechanical means, including information storage and retrieval systems, without written permission from the author, except for the use of brief quotations in a book review.

Cover art by www.getcovers.com

This is a work of fiction. Names, characters, places and incidents are the product of the author's imagination or are used fictitiously, and any resemblance to actual persons living, or dead, business establishments, events or locales is entirely coincidental.

These books were written in the UK and edited in British English, where some spelling, grammar and word usage will be different to US English.

Created with Vellum

For Tara <3

Happy Christmas :)

CHAPTER 1

The sea charged up the shore in frothy white waves. My glass café door rattled with the fierce breeze as I unlocked it. I certainly wasn't expecting many customers that morning. It was four days until Christmas, and I guessed most people were inland looking for last minute presents at one of the shopping centres in Bristol, or doing the sensible thing, cosying up in front of the fireplace with a good book. I rubbed my hands together as I scanned the bay. The seaside resort looked a lot different to how it did on a gentle summer's day. A few people still braved a walk along the prom, the type that did this every morning come rain or shine, holding onto their coats as the wind fought to derobe them. A dog charged across the sand, chasing a ball that had been caught by the wind, its ears flapping up and down.

I switched the sign on the door from closed, to open and turned around, smiling at the Christmas decorations I had put up. To the left of the French doors was a Christmas tree covered in multicoloured lights. The scent of the needles reminded me of childhood excitement, of waiting for Santa and putting a carrot out for Rudolf. My tree was a bit lacking in hanging ornaments, as I was waiting for the Christmas Fair, so I could buy a few there rather than traipsing out of town. I'd found a small collection in the attic room of the large Victorian house I'd inherited from my Grandma. When I'd moved to Branden Bay earlier that year, Mrs Jessup, my next-door neighbour, had told me that when she was a girl, Grandma's house was a café. With no other career on the horizon, I'd followed my love of baking and opened 'Connie's Café'.

"Morning, lovey."

I turned around as Lynn walked into the café from the opposite end of the property. She smiled at me as she donned her apron. Lynn ran a spiritualist church in an old scout hut that backed onto my garden. It wasn't just the house I'd inherited from Grandma, I'd also inherited the gift for seeing the dead. Lynn had been helping me to cope with this unwanted new skill. Unfortunately, I'd always been petrified of ghosts.

"Morning," I said with a smile.

"How are you?" she asked.

"I'm feeling festive," I said.

"And who wouldn't in here, it looks beautiful."

"I just wish we could all be together on Christmas Day. I was gutted this morning when Dannie left to go to her parents' house." Dannie was one of my lodgers and had lived with me for around six months, during which time I'd become quite close to her and she was like the younger sister I never had. She did my accounts and looked after a lot of my administration, as well as taking a bookkeeping course up at the local technical college.

"We all promised you that next year, we'll have a big one here in the café." Lynn smiled at me as she busied herself behind the counter.

I nodded. "I've always loved Christmas and those I spent here with Grandma were the very best."

"And you'll be wanting to spent time with your folks."

I smiled. That was true I'd not seen my parents for two years as they'd been travelling the world on a trip of a lifetime and were due home on Christmas Eve.

I heard a loud meow and looked at my feet to see my ginger cat. I'd taken her in soon after I had moved to Branden Bay from London and named her Constance after my Grandma, as she had similar bushy hair and green eyes.

I picked her up. “Connie cat, it’s going to be our first ever Christmas together. Maybe you will have turkey?” I said to her as she purred in my arms.

Constance only ate salmon and certainly shunned anything that came from a tin or a packet. And I always dished up her steamed fish on one of Grandma’s china plates.

“What are the specials today?” Lynn asked.

I looked at my board and pointed. “The sandwich platter includes turkey and cranberry, or avocado and cranberry for the vegetarian option. I’ve baked way too many mince pies, so they’re on offer. And I’ve the Rudolf cupcakes for the kids.” I’d made the small sweet cakes and topped them with a fondant reindeer face, a red nose and poked chocolate twigs in the top for the antlers. “Although I’m not sure how busy we’ll be. Not many people will brave the seafront in this weather.” I gestured outside.

Constance jumped to the floor as the café door opened and Annie came in. She pushed the door shut behind her then turned around. “It’s wicked out there, I hope it calms down before Friday.” She popped by the café every morning for coffee, on her way to work.

"Are you busy?" I asked her.

"Yes, as Friday is the Christmas Fair." She passed me her travel mug.

"Of course, I'm hoping to pick up some tree decorations."

"We've two venders with decorations, so you're in luck. But I'm totally rushed off my feet co-ordinating it. It's a bit of a shock to come back to, after my Caribbean holiday."

"Andrew is no doubt making you pay with hard work after he allowed you to take extended leave."

Annie laughed. "You're not wrong, he's a great boss but he makes us work hard. I've only got Christmas day off this year. But, the fair must go on," she gestured her hand up, mimicking her boss with a laugh.

"I love the Christmas Fair," Lynn said. "With it being on a Friday this year, it's going to be extra busy."

"Do you want me to make some festive cookies to sell?" I asked Annie. "With the weather being as it is, I won't be rushed off my feet serving all day. I can easily make a few batches up."

"That would be amazing. Could you bring the cart as the kiosks are full."

"Sure." I had a cart out the back, which we used for selling cookies during town events.

"Great, I'll sort a price for you with Andrew," Annie said.

"What else have you there?" I asked.

"Toy stalls, food stalls, themed attractions, a Santa's Grotto and of course the choir." She turned to Lynn. "Aren't you singing with them this year?"

Lynn sighed. "Yes, before we turn on the Christmas tree lights. I wish I'd never agreed to them practicing in the hut. I got dragged in when someone dropped out."

"I'm definitely coming to watch," I said with a grin.

Constance meowed and rubbed against Lynn's legs.

"You haven't heard us. It sounds pretty awful," Lynn said with a sigh.

"What time are you on?" I asked.

"Six o'clock." Lynn puffed out.

"What's wrong?" Annie asked.

"I'm no singer and it sounds awful. Those with the best voices keep leaving."

I laughed. "I can't wait."

"Constance sings better than that lot," Lynn said.

Constance mowed loudly.

Lynn bent down and picked her up.

"I'm sure you tip the balance, Lynn," Annie said.

"I think it's a lost cause." Lynn stroked Constance's head.

"Have you heard from your parents?" Annie asked me.

I passed over her cappuccino. "Yes, they've a flight booked and are landing in Exeter Friday night, then staying there as it lands in the early hours. They'll hire a car and drive up."

"So, they'll arrive Christmas Eve, how wonderful," Lynn said.

My other lodger, Jeff sloped into the room wearing an Avengers T-shirt. He scratched his scrappy beard, which matched the sandy coloured hair on his head. "Any chance of a coffee to go? I'm late for work. I've taken on an extra shift." Jeff was part way through a science masters which he studied in Bristol and had a part-time job up at the local D.I.Y. store.

"Of course," I said as I reached for a takeout cup.

"It's quiet around here without Dannie," he said.

"I know. It seems odd with just us here."

"Are you sure you should be going to work? You look whacked out," Lynn asked him.

"I'm tired after last night's ghost hunt up at the castle."

As well as attending university, and a part-time job, Jeff was running ghost hunts. He was saving for a house and already had a tidy sum in his bank account.

"You'll have to watch out else you'll burn yourself

out!" Annie said as she took a sip of her coffee and looked outside, as if dreading the final stretch of her walk to work.

"Oh, bother," Lynn said staring at her mobile phone.

Constance jumped from her arms to the floor.

"What?" Annie asked.

"Rosemary has left the choir," Lynn said. "She was a really decent singer and the soloist. She's one of the founding members."

"Maybe you can do the solo?" Jeff said to Lynn as he took the filled takeout cup from my hand.

"Not likely," Lynn said. "I've asked Rosemary to pop in on her way to the charity shop, I'll make her a spiced hot chocolate to see if that calms her down." Lynn turned to the coffee machine.

"I'll be off then," Jeff said as he yawned again.

"Me too, see you tomorrow," Annie said. As she opened the door she let my neighbour in, before waving goodbye.

After serving Mrs Jessup her morning tea and a cinnamon muffin, I looked up to see Rosemary come in through the café doors. She was a member of the local Ladies' Society and had recently started volunteering in a charity shop I was involved with called *Cat Lovers*. It was in the High Street and sold second hand goods with a few novelty cat items. Rosemary looked incredibly flustered and pulled her scarf from her head after I shut the door behind her.

"Thank you, Becky." She walked up to Lynn. "I've had enough of the choir, I'm not saying I'm leaving forever, but I need a break," she said. "It was the final straw last week when I argued with Deloris." She brushed the hair out of her eyes. "I've been getting myself completely worked up about it this week. I just don't want to go. And then I thought, I'm in my forties, I jolly well don't have to do anything I don't want to. I spent twenty years with the stress of a business and when I sold it, I expected to have a quiet life. I certainly don't need the constant argy-bargy. It's supposed to be a *hobby*."

Wow, I thought. Rosemary had always appeared to be a passive woman. I'd not seen her so vocal.

"There aren't enough of us," Lynn said. "And Christmas is such a happy time. Maybe when you've calmed down and had this lovely hot chocolate."

"No. I've had it. I'm sorry but I won't be singing for months, I need to calm down." Rosemary looked at me. "What about you, Becky? I'm sure I read that you studied performing arts."

"Yes, she's a trained singer," Lynn added and smiled at me as if she was proud.

"I had lessons as part of my performing arts degree, but I'm no soprano."

'I've heard you singing around the house," Mrs

Jessup said from her table, clearly listening in as she lifted her gaze from her latest novel. "I've heard you through the bathroom wall."

"You're coming," Lynn said gesturing at me.

"No," I protested.

"Please, dear, it'll take the guilt away for me," Rosemary said. "I work for you for free in the charity shop. I've told my Keith that I'm done with the choir, and he was so relieved because he's fed up with me complaining about it. So I can't go back now."

"What's the issue?" I asked, intrigued at what could be so stressful about singing a few Christmas carols.

"Deloris wants to do the solo and was grumpy with me taking that spot," Rosemary said.

"Deloris can be difficult," Lynn added.

"Why not step back and let her do it?" I asked.

"It's not that simple. There are certain dynamics at the choir," Rosemary said. "She would be enormously smug about it. But you would be perfect. You're fresh and new. She's always lovely to new people. Before they get to know her."

"I'm not taking no for an answer," Lynn said. "You've been complaining that you're bored in the evenings. And you've been moping around, missing that boyfriend of yours. And you love Christmas."

I looked at Lynn. I had been kind of sulking about not seeing H over Christmas. And Lynn had helped me out with the café for months before I started paying her. She looked desperate. It was true I did love Christmas and singing. I didn't have a good enough excuse to say no.

"Come on it'll be fun," she said clearly sensing me caving in.

"You weren't painting it as fun five minutes ago. And neither were you, Rosemary."

"You'll love it," Rosemary said as she nodded frantically before sipping her hot chocolate.

I was not convinced as Lynn showed Rosemary to a table. I listened as Rosemary tried to recruit Lynn to Branden Bay Ladies' Society. I'd been meaning to join myself. I left them to it and went to the kitchen to check that I had enough ingredients for the cookies I intended to bake for the Christmas Fair.

When I returned to the café, Lynn was wiping down the table she had been sharing with Rosemary, who had since left.

"So you're in?" Lynn asked me.

"Yes. How many are in the choir?"

"Well, there'll be me and you," Lynn started counting on her fingers as she went. "Then Fred, Suzy, Karen, Mark, Tracey and finally Deloris."

"Is that it? It's hardly a choir. I thought I'd blend into the background. Even if I join, it's only an octet!"

"People have been leaving. The atmosphere is

often tense, but you've such a great sense of presence, I'm sure your energy and beautiful aura will liven the place up."

"You're not exactly selling it to me, Lynn," I said with a sigh.

Constance meowed at my feet and I picked her up.

"What are we singing?" I asked.

"A mixture of traditional carols and Christmas songs."

I smiled. At least the tunes were bound to cheer me up. *How bad could it be?* I thought as I refilled Mrs Jessup's' tea pot. We were just singing a few festive favourites.

CHAPTER 2

I filled a large plastic tub with mince pies to take to the choir practice, for all Lynn had said, I was looking forward to singing Christmas carols and was in good spirits.

Constance meowed at my feet as I went to the back door situated in my kitchen.

I looked down. "You want to come too?" I laughed, imagining Constance joining in. From what Lynn had said, my vocal cat would fit in well with the wailing voices of the choir.

"Come on then," I said to Constance as I opened the door.

I pulled my coat tight to my body as we ran down the garden. The wind whistled around the bare branches of the apple tree, through which I could see the moon. It was quite eerie. At the end of the garden, I pulled the wooden gate which creaked open. The spiritualist church was run from an old scout hut and I followed Constance up the wooden steps and then pushed the door open.

As I entered, the choir members turned to look at us. We were on time, but it seemed everyone else was early. Clearly eager to get on with their singing.

"Welcome to the choir, Becky. I'm Fred, the choir master." He was tall with a shock of dark hair, a mix of black and grey. He wore a paisley sweater with a green shirt underneath and had an air of authority about him. "Meet the chorus." He gestured around the room.

"Hi," I said with a small wave, balancing the pie filled tub with my other hand. I felt as if I was the new girl on her first day at school.

Constance meowed at my feet.

"Oh," I said looking down at her then back up. "I hope you don't mind me bringing Constance. She does like to follow me everywhere."

A raven-haired woman approached me. "I read about her in the newspaper, wasn't she abducted last month?" She didn't leave me space to answer. "No wonder she wants to be with you. The poor little mite." She bent down and stroked Constance as my cat arched her back. "You're a beautiful puss-cat." She picked her up and smiled at me. "I'm Suzy, by the way. We've just been hearing from Lynn that you're a brilliant singer."

I shot a look at my guilty looking friend.

Lynn gave a small smile, then approached me with her hand held out. "I'll put the mince pies in the kitchen for you, lovey."

A large woman, dressed in a red dress with printed images of snowmen on it and thick green tights stood in the corner. She had one hand on her hip and the other gesturing upwards. She was older than the others there, looking around late seventies, whereas the rest of the choir seemed to be in their forties. She gave me a hard stare and began to sing a scale. I frowned. She sang somewhat on the sharp side and as she climbed up the scale, the notes sharpened with each increment.

Eek, I thought. *This is going to be interesting.*

Suzy gave me an apologetic smile and lowered her voice. "Deloris tells us all that she used to sing opera and that she was classically trained."

I put a hand up to my ear. "Really?"

'Hmm,' Suzy said. "To be honest, I have my doubts."

Constance gave a pitiful meow.

I was pretty convinced that Deloris must be lying and that wasn't anything to do with any psychic power, it was because the woman was seriously off key.

Suzy smiled. "I'm glad you're here, it's nice to have someone so young in the fold. I'll introduce you to everyone else."

Suzy led me to a blond man as she held Constance in her arms, "This is Mark."

"General handyman and dog's body," he said with a laugh. "I'm trying to set up my own maintenance business, so if you know anyone local who needs work done. No job is too small, or too big." He reached into his pocket and handed me a card with *Mark the odd Job Man,* written on it and a cartoon style picture of a hammer.

I took the card. "Thank you. I often need things doing in my house."

Tracey approached us. I recognised her from the seafront pub, *The Branden Arms*.

Constance meowed and jumped to the floor from Suzy's clutches. Tracey was used to seeing Constance when I visited the pub she ran with her husband.

"You brighten the place up, Constance." Tracey bent down and stroked her. "It's nice to have a local celebrity in the choir." She looked up at me.

I laughed. "A lot of what is written in the newspaper about us is exaggerated." My friend Izzy was a reporter for a weekly newspaper, which covered the whole of the Southwest of England and had covered all of my cases. She had a way of making me sound like I had a mastermind brain in her articles, when in truth, I often stumbled around the investigations, relying heavily on contact with the other side for information. I sighed, I missed Izzy. She was out of town for the season, visiting her parents in London who were over for the holiday period, from Sweden. She had assured me she would be back for the New Year celebrations.

"Introduce Becky to Deloris," Tracey said to Suzy as she stood up. "It might shut her up."

As we approached Deloris, she had moved onto her arpeggios, which were even more excruciating to the ear. She put her hand up as if to say, *don't interrupt*.

Constance gave a low meow from behind me which clashed with the woman's voice.

Suzy steered me towards a woman who wore a grey skirt and matching cardigan. She was putting a compact disc into a music system.

"This is Karen," Suzy said.

Karen gave me a warm smile. "It's nice to meet you." She shuddered as she pushed her mousy coloured hair behind her ears. She looked around the room and then back at Constance. "Although, I'm not too keen on the occult."

I laughed. "Me neither."

"I find it a bit spooky in here," Karen said.

"Don't worry," Lynn said as she approached us.

"This church is not haunted. There are no sprits here unless I call them up and I've no intention of doing that this evening."

"And don't pay any attention to what you read in the Gazette, it's exaggerated," I said trying to put Karen at ease. I knew exactly what it was like to be afraid of spirits. I shuddered remembering the times I'd seen ghostly beings and really hoped I would not be seeing another, any time soon.

Karen continued. "We used to practice up at the Ladies' Society Hall." She looked at Deloris. "But not all of our members liked it up there."

Tracey joined us still with Constance in her arms and frowned as Deloris belted out a top note. "For pity's sake."

"She says she once caused a glass to smash, with only her voice," Suzy said.

"I can believe that," I said, worrying that my eardrums would burst.

"More like someone threw it at her, in an attempt to shut her up," Tracey said.

I laughed, a little bit too loud as Deloris stopped and gave me a hard stare.

Constance jumped to the floor and hissed.

"Come along, let's warm up," Fred said with a swift clap of his hands.

"Don't worry about him," Tracey said. "He's the headmaster of Branden Bay Primary School and he treats us all as if we've just arrived for morning assembly. But he's a nice guy."

We stood in a line before him.

"La," he sang and we all followed the note as he led us precariously up the scale.

I don't mean to be unkind, but it sounded awful. The main problem being that Deloris insisted on singing a whole octave, plus part of a semitone, higher than the rest of us. Constance wailed at the same time, but I wasn't sure if anyone else noticed that she was joining in, as Deloris was so loud. I groaned. What had I let myself in for? Was I going to be publicly humiliated? Maybe I could fake a case of laryngitis before the Christmas Fair sing-out.

Once Fred had finished the warmup, he rubbed his hands together. "I've decided that our Christmas set will be, *O Little Town of Bethlehem*, *Away in a Manger*, *Oh Come all ye faithful.* And the songs will be, *When Santa got stuck up the Chimney* and *Jingle Bells.*" He looked directly at Deloris. "If time permits, Deloris and myself will perform a duet of Ding Dong Merrily on High."

Oh dear, I thought. That was a duet I did not want to be subjected to.

"Followed by my solo," Deloris said, smoothing down her festive dress. "The First Noel."

"I think we should drop duets and solos now that Rosemary has left," Mark said.

"I agree, I don't think solos or duets are a good idea," Tracey said in a loud voice staring at Deloris. "With such a small chorus I thought we decided that it's all about the audience joining in, rather than a show."

"True," Karen added in a small voice and flashed a nervous glance at Deloris.

"Speak up woman," Deloris said staring at the timid singer.

'I didn't think we were doing duets," Karen said with a deep blush.

Suzy exchanged a worried glance with Fred. "Maybe we could compromise on one duet?"

"There will be no compromise," Deloris said. "I'm doing a duet with Fred and my operatic solo." She smiled at me. "With me being professionally trained, the performance will be a resounding success."

It was clear from the look on the faces of the rest of the chorus that everyone was horrified by the prospect of a Deloris solo.

"We have to entertain." Deloris' voice had a determined edge to it. "I want to sing."

"I can understand that," Mark said. "But maybe we should audition for the solo and duet spots?" He looked directly at me. "We need the best singers."

"I'll have you know, I was trained at The Royal Academy of Music," Deloris said.

"So, you've said," Lynn whispered.

"Many times," Tracey grumbled.

Deloris did not hear their mumbled comments.

Tracey gestured at me. "If the newspapers reported correctly, Becky here is also professionally trained. Maybe we should hear her sing and put a vote to it?"

I groaned. I'd been expecting a fun evening singing Christmas songs and now I was potentially being thrown into battle-of-the-voices. "I don't want to do a solo. It's been ages since I've performed."

"Quite," Deloris said. "Vocal cords must be regularly exercised. My coach at The Royal Academy of Music said..."

"Shall we get along with the practice?" Suzy interrupted looking at the clock on the wall. "This is our last rehearsal before the Christmas Fair sing-out. And the first event of our Christmas programme."

"First?" I asked glancing at Lynn as I frowned.

"Yes," Fred said. "We have Friday evening at the fair and Christmas Eve by Candlelight up at the Church, for the family service. As we do every year."

"My parents are coming home on Christmas Eve," I said frowning at Lynn.

"I'm sure they'll be over the moon to watch you up at the church. What a wonderful homecoming," Lynn said with a smile.

"The choir was first set up in Christmas 1995 to raise funds for our church," Tracey said.

"Enough of the history lesson, let's get on with it," Mark said. "Otherwise, we'll have no show at all."

Fred distributed the song sheets. "Keep these for the sing-outs, I've written your names at the top. The first page is the running order and then the rest are the words. We don't have time to learn them off by heart. Especially not our new member."

I stared at the page to see my name at the top, reminding me of being in the school choir.

"Can I suggest we work quickly through the group songs," Deloris said. "And then Fred and I can stay behind and practice our duet before we go over my solo."

"Suits me," Mark said. "At least the rest of us won't have to stay and listen."

Tracey laughed.

"You're an extremely rude man," Deloris said. "And you're not much better, Tracey. I must say I am surprised."

Mark exchanged a look with Tracey and then gave a short cough. "I'm not being rude, I've got my first handyman job in the morning, and I need to get up early."

"We'll start with – *O little Town of Bethlehem.*" Fred paused. "Karen?"

Karen pressed play on the C.D. player hooked up to a P.A. system.

We began singing the first carol. It was messy at best, painful at worst. I stared at Lynn who smiled back at me apologetically.

When we'd finished, Deloris flicked her white hair from her shoulder. "Some of you were flat."

"We were all flat compared to you," Mark said. "I've said it before, you sing too sharp."

"What on earth do you know? You're a school caretaker." She paused. "Oh, sorry I forgot – you got the sack. A handyman."

The colour of Mark's face deepened to maroon, and he squinted as he stared back at her. Keeping his lips pressed together as if he was scared he would spout something that was inappropriate for a choir practice.

"I, however, was trained at The Royal Academy of Music," Deloris continued.

The room gave a collective groan.

"If she says that one more time..." Mark said through gritted teeth.

Deloris glared at him and then pointed forcefully at me. "She'll tell you I'm in key."

Everyone stared at me. I gulped, I had nowhere to go. I toyed with the idea of lying but when I lied, I usually got myself into deep trouble, so I went with a dumbed down truth. "Maybe you were a smidgen sharp?"

Deloris placed her hands on her hips. "I knew it. You're here to push me out and put yourself into the solo position." She gestured at me. "You're just a career carol singer."

"A what? That's ridiculous," I said.

Constance hissed and bushed out her fur.

Lynn bent down and grabbed her, she was probably just as worried as me, that my cat was about to launch herself at Deloris.

"More like you're the career caroller," Mark said pointing at Deloris. "If it wasn't for you, Rosemary wouldn't have left. She has an amazing voice."

"Oh Mark, you just fancied her," Deloris said.

"No, I did not. I'm a married man."

"It's not stopped you before," Deloris said.

"You're bang out of order," Mark shouted.

"Will you please remain calm," Fred ordered.

Suzy put her arm on Mark's as if to restrain him. He appeared flabbergasted.

Deloris turned back to me. "From what I've read in the newspaper, it's clear you're a fake and a fraud." Her face became so red it near matched her dress.

Lynn held onto a struggling Constance.

I took a step backwards taking in her viscous response, not knowing quite how to respond.

Lynn passed my cat to me then approached

Deloris. "Lovey, you've got it wrong. I twisted Becky's arm to get her to come along. She didn't even want to be here. If you attack her, we won't have enough singers for our performances."

"Maybe we should cancel our shows," Karen said looking worried. She blinked rapidly as if she was having trouble dealing with the tension in the room.

"And why do we have to practice in here anyway?" Deloris gestured around the room. "The acoustics are dull and flat. It was much better up at the hall."

Lynn put an affectionate hand on her arm. "Take a few breaths, dear."

"You lot will be the death of me," Deloris said then took a few shallow breaths.

"I thought you didn't like the Ladies' Society Hall," Tracey said. "You felt Rosemary ruled the roost up there and it was too much of a walk?"

"That amateur was never a threat to me and I'm sure one of you could have given me a lift." She gestured around the room.

"Order, order," Fred called out and stepped forward.

"All I want is for us to put on a good show." Deloris looked at Karen. "And we've been collecting for the donkey sanctuary as I suggested for a year now. We need to take this seriously."

"Come on, let's get on with it," Mark said with a gruff voice. "Otherwise, I'm out of here."

And I'll be right behind you, I thought looking at him as I stroked Constance.

"Away in a Manger," Fred called out.

Karen returned to the C.D. player and selected the correct track.

We continued without complaints, yet it was still woefully out of tune. I sang with Constance in my arms as I knew the words to these well-known songs, I had no need to follow the printed words. But I found it difficult to sing in tune myself, with Deloris belting her notes out, off key. I looked around and saw Lynn with a finger in her ear, trying to hear her own voice. I could not do that since I was keeping a tight grip on my cat.

After an hour of going over the carols and songs, we thankfully stopped.

Fred rubbed his hands together. "Let's have refreshments and then myself and Deloris will stay back to practice our duet."

"And you can hear my solo, Fred," Deloris said with a flick of her hair.

"Help me make the teas," Lynn whispered to me.

I followed her to the kitchen having passed Constance to Tracey. "Thanks Lynn. But I'm not going to go forward with the choir."

"But it'll fall apart without you," she said.

"Oh, come on. I've only been to one rehearsal and they're not ready to be heard in public. I think the best thing is for it to be disbanded. If you and I leave, we'll be doing them all a huge favour. Karen and Mark seem quite happy for it to end as well."

"But we're letting the donkeys down. We've donated a thousand pounds so far and they really could do with the extra funds, for medication and food."

"Lynn, you're making me feel bad," I said. "I've only been a part of the choir for an hour!"

"Give it some thought. Let me do the teas and you can hand out your delicious mince pies. It's not usually as tense as it is tonight. Get to know the others, they're a lovely bunch."

When we returned to the main room with the refreshments, the choir members had pulled a couple of tables together and were sitting in silence. I handed out the mince pies I'd baked. They were well received, and I even got a smile from Deloris as she put the pie into her mouth and closed her blue eyes as she munched on the crumbly pastry and spicy fruit mixture.

"Well, my dear," she said dabbing her mouth with a napkin. "Your singing may leave a lot to be desired, but you can certainly bake."

"Huh!" Mark said from across the room. "Becky has a great voice."

"I also thought Becky sang beautifully," Suzy said giving me a smile before looking thoughtfully at her mince pie. "Is this one of your grandmother's recipes?" she asked.

"Yes. I made the mixture myself. It's not shop bought."

Constance jumped from Tracey onto my lap and purred.

"Ah," Deloris said. "A secret recipe. I think I'll pop into your café and sample the other delights you have on offer." She looked at me as she took another bite.

I groaned inside and Constance hissed.

"Do you mind if I have another?" Fred asked.

"Help yourself," I said. "I'm not taking the left-overs home, as I'll make a fresh batch tomorrow."

Tracey chatted away to Mark in a low voice, nodding at Deloris who was speaking to Karen. Suzy sat with Fred but also stared at Deloris. Constance gave a loud meow from my lap, so I stroked her to calm her down.

Fred stood up. "Right then, what outfits are we going to wear to the fair?"

"I quite like Deloris' dress. Where do you get it?" Tracey asked.

"I ordered it on-line, it arrived just before I came." She smoothed down her festive attire with her hands.

"I think with it being chilly, we should wear Christmas jumpers," Suzy suggested.

Fred nodded. "Good idea, Suzy." He stood up. "Deloris, let's go over the duet. I'll see you all at the sing-out on Friday," he said looking at me with a smile.

"Oh, yes, of course," I said but I didn't care what Lynn said, I had no intention of singing with those people, ever again. To ease my conscience, I decided to make a sizeable donation to the donkey sanctuary.

CHAPTER 3

Constance jumped onto my bedroom windowsill and hissed. It was gone ten at night and the light was still on at the spiritualist hut. I saw the outlines of two heads through the window.

They're staying late, I thought. But luckily, I couldn't hear any singing from my bedroom, which pleased me.

I pulled the curtains closed and Constance jumped onto my bed. The room had been mine as a child, when I'd visited Grandma during every school holiday. It was huge and had doubled up as my playroom. The grandest bedroom was the one at the front of the house, with views of the bay and promenade, but Dannie slept in there and while she was away with her family, I'd made the room up for my parents to use. I still had another spare room which

Dannie could sleep in, if she returned before they left. To be honest I was not aware of my parents' future plans, their own house was let out to tenants.

As I laid back on my bed, I remembered how we used to sing Christmas songs as a family. My parents loved the duet, *It's Cold Outside*. Even though they were both lawyers by trade, both of them had beautiful singing voices and had met through their university's chorus. And Grandma had the sweetest voice of all, being a professional actress and singer. I sighed as Constance settled herself at the end of my bed. I missed my parents and was so pleased that it was only two days until I would see them again. I wondered what they would make of my boyfriend and his family. I'd become really close to his parents, Carol and Paul. I drifted off to sleep imagining future family get-togethers.

An hour later, I woke with a start and stared at my clock, bleary eyed. I could hear a woman singing *The First Noel.*

"Deloris? Surely not," I said aloud to Constance who stood at the end of the bed with her coat bushed out. Clearly, my cat was not impressed with the night-time singing either. *The wind must be blowing it over from the hut,* I thought as I could hear it quite loudly. I sat up and felt a fizz of static up my back and down my arms.

I frowned. Experiencing static was often the sign

that a spirit was close by, or that there was imminent danger. I suspected that the person in imminent danger was Deloris, as I didn't rate her chances of survival once I got over there and told her to shut up.

"Be quiet," I shouted as I jumped out of bed and pulled back the curtains with a force. I hadn't taken a shine to Deloris and didn't know how the rest of the choir had put up with her for so long. This was the final straw.

The singing became louder.

"For goodness' sake," I said. "Stop, just stop!" I turned to a wailing Constance. "She'll have to finish up and go home. It's getting on for midnight. Those high tones will wake the whole of the neighbourhood up." I tried to calm Constance as she gave a long wailing meow. I wondered whether Deloris was singing through a microphone, it was so loud. "Come on, Constance," I said to my cat. I pulled a sweater over the top of my pyjamas and fetched a pair of boots from my wardrobe.

As I went out of the room I was met by a yawning Jeff. "What's all the noise about?"

"That's what I need to sort out."

"I heard you two through the wall."

"It's not me and Constance!" I shook my head. Surely Jeff didn't think that my singing could be that bad. "It's coming from the spiritualist hut."

Jeff rubbed his eyes, "I'll come with you."

"It's such awful singing, I can't sleep with that racket."

"Singing? All I could hear was you shouting and Constance meowing," Jeff muttered.

I thought that he must be half asleep if he couldn't hear the carol being belted into the night. Mind you, Deloris' singing did resemble a cat crying out in pain.

"Just come on," I said as I heard Deloris sing a long drawn-out *Noel*.

Constance and Jeff followed me down the stairs, through the kitchen and out of the back door.

I stomped down the garden, across the wet grass.

Constance bounded ahead, jumped onto the garden wall and hissed. I opened the gate and walked through. We went up the steps to the hut.

My hand fizzed as I touched the handle and static raced up my arm. I turned to Jeff. "I feel like something bad is going to happen."

"Boss, it looks like you're tapping into something paranormal," Jeff said in a groggy voice. "And look at Constance."

Constance hissed and her bushed-out fur made her look twice her usual size.

"I'll pop back and get my gear," Jeff said.

"We haven't got time, I need to tell her to keep quiet."

"There's no noise apart from the wind, the sea and you," Jeff said.

I pushed open the door.

"Can you see anything?" Jeff asked.

Static raged through my body as I stared at the scene. The singing continued and yes, I could see Deloris, but she was glowing and flickering on and off. On the floor was her body, gazing lifeless at the ceiling with a mince pie stuffed into her mouth.

Deloris' spirit stopped her vocal assault and she stared at me. I heard her say, *I want to sing. I just want to sing.*

JEFF RETURNED to the house and called Lynn, while I sat on the steps of the hut clutching Constance to me as the static subsided. Deloris' spirit had disappeared while her body remained lifeless on the spiritualist hut floor.

I stood up when Lynn arrived. The three of us stared at Deloris' body on the floor, from the doorway.

"We really need to call an ambulance," Lynn said.

"Why? She's dead," I said. "I saw her spirit." The odd spasm still ticked in my hands.

"I'll call emergency services," Jeff said. "They'll get the police and an ambulance here."

Lynn called Fred to find out what time he had left Deloris and he said that he'd finished at half nine. I noted that this was before I'd seen two people through the window of the hut. Was he mistaken? Or had someone else joined Deloris?

The ambulance arrived first and the paramedics rushed in, checking Deloris' vitals and then stepped back unsurprisingly announcing that she was dead. They waited with us for the police.

I groaned as I saw the flashing lights and Detective Chief Inspector Bradley Harris, get out of his vehicle. He was far from fond of me. He used to work for the vice squad in Bristol and started his career undercover. Because of this, he looked more like a gangster than a policeman. He hated me treading on his investigations. He'd recently transferred to Branden Bay with his co-worker and they were expecting triplets. I'd heard that Brad was supposed to be on light duties waiting for his paternity leave and was suffering from stress. But he was clearly still working. I was sure his mental state was more to do with impeding fatherhood than his workload. Apparently, the pregnancy wasn't planned, and Brad had never wanted children. I didn't want to be the one to tip him over the edge, as I knew he was not a fan of mine and while I was always genuine, I knew I pushed him to the limits of his patience.

"What are you doing here?" Brad growled as he reached me.

Another police car drew up behind his parked vehicle.

"I was with Deloris, the victim, earlier on at choir practice and discovered the body."

"So how did she die?"

"We don't know," Lynn replied.

"We found her on the floor with the mince pie in her mouth," I said.

Brad breathed out slowly then called out to the paramedics. "Any sign of injury?"

They shook their heads.

"I think she had health issues," Lynn said.

"But the mince pie is curious, people don't usually put a whole one in their mouth," I said.

"She did say she liked the mince pies," Lynn said to Brad. "Earlier on this evening, Deloris said Becky was an amazing baker. Maybe she ate too many?"

Brad turned to me. "Or the pie was poisoned. So, the murder weapon was baked by you?"

"Hey, it's a pie, not a weapon. And it's hardly my fault!"

"I ate one of those pies earlier, Inspector," Lynn said.

"And me," I said.

"I had one at home, and I'm still alive," Jeff said.

"Great observation skills," Brad replied with a sarcastic tone.

"The pies were scrummylicious," Lynn added. "The fruit mix is so original."

"I'm not here to swap recipes." Brad walked towards the paramedics. "What's the cause of death?"

"We don't know, you'll need the doctor to examine her. We'll take her in, unless you think this is a crime scene. She appears to be early eighties. I would check her medical records to look for any health issues."

Brad nodded. "Possibly natural causes then." He eyed me, looked back at Deloris and then back to me again. I could see he wanted to ask me something. He grabbed my arm and took me outside and out of earshot of everyone else.

Once on the steps he hesitated then fidgeted. He reminded me of a man too nervous to ask a woman out on a date. But I knew that clearly was not the reason. I felt it inside my chest – Brad wanted to know if I'd seen Deloris' ghost. But he always said I should keep out of it, that I talked a load of rubbish, but I could see concern in his eyes and felt with my psychic sense that he had a gut feeling that something was up with this death. After all, even though he may not always catch the killer before I did, he was still an award-winning detective and often on the right track. This was one proud man and the silence between us became thick.

I decided to put him out of his misery. "I know you don't believe a word I say, but I saw Deloris' ghost this evening, and the sound of her singing woke me up and led me to her body. I think she may have been killed."

Brad said nothing but took a deep breath and his eyes bore into mine. I saw his jaw flex and the head of his snake tattoo moved on his neck as his vein twitched. "I'll see you at noon in your cafe," he said in a gruff voice. "Now get back home."

I blinked, as awful as Brad had been to me in the past, I felt strangely complimented.

Jeff and I said goodbye to Lynn, who was asked to wait while they moved the body.

I sat on my window seat in my bedroom, watching the scene until the light went out in the hut.

Poor Deloris, I thought. Even though she was annoying, it seemed a bit harsh for someone to kill her. Although, Lynn had said she was suffering with health issues, the vision of my mince pie in her mouth troubled me. It didn't look like she had been eating it, it looked as if it had been stuffed inside. She didn't come across as the sort of lady who would eat a mince pie whole. Maybe someone had tried to shut her up with it. I felt a shock of static and a glimmer of light in the hut. I rubbed my eyes as Constance wailed and the singing resumed.

Ding dong merrily on high... Deloris' spirit sang.

Whatever the situation, I knew in my heart of hearts that I was going to have to listen to this every night, unless I found out how Deloris had died.

CHAPTER 4

In the morning, Jeff knocked and then opened my bedroom door, he was wearing his superhero dressing gown.

I peered at him from my bed. "Is everything okay?"

Constance jumped from the end of my bed and approached him for a stroke.

"The news is in," Jeff said. "Someone's posted on *Spotted in Branden Bay,* that Deloris died from eating your mince pie, which gave her a heart attack."

"Brilliant," I said. "Not a great advert for the café."

"Are we going to investigate? I wish I'd been more awake last night and realised you were seeing a spirit from the start. The amount of hours I've been working is insane."

"I've no choice, Deloris' spirit kept me and Constance awake all night with her awful singing."

"Great," Jeff said with a grin on his face.

I would have had a go at him as I didn't think it was *great* myself, but it was nice to see Jeff smile again. He was recovering from a very nasty breakup from his first real girlfriend.

Constance gave a low meow.

"She must have been murdered." I yawned. "Otherwise, why is she still here?"

"We'll stake the hut out tonight," Jeff said as he picked up my cat. "And get some answers."

My mobile phone rang. It was Lynn.

"Lovey, the choir are meeting up at The Branden Arms this morning, for breakfast before opening time, to pay their respects to Deloris. I thought you might want to come?"

"I certainly do. Considering Brad is coming over to my place at twelve." It would be good to have some observations to give him. "I'm shutting the cafe today, we need to nip this one in the bud. Word is out that Deloris died after eating my mince pie, so I'm not expecting many customers." I wanted the background on these choir members. "I don't want my Christmas to be ruined by an out-of-tune ghost."

Jeff left the room to have a shower, he was off to work for another early shift at the D.I.Y. store.

My phone dinged with a text, it was from my

boyfriend, H. I groaned, he had probably heard what had happened. H was also known as Detective Sergeant Henry Blake and was often pleading with me to leave investigations to the police. Maybe Brad had told him about me finding the body. But no, I sat up and smiled, it wasn't about death, H was planning to pop over and see me the following evening. I was extremely happy, we could go to the Christmas Fair together and the sing-out would surely be cancelled. I texted back to say I was looking forward to seeing him and jumped out of bed to get ready for breakfast at the pub.

"MAYBE IT WAS NATURAL CAUSES," Lynn said as we reached The Branden Arms pub, with Constance in tow. "Deloris was always telling us about her dodgy ticker."

I rapped on the door and Tracey let us in. She ran the pub with her husband, Roger.

The other members of the choir were already there. They were all smiling and sat at three tables pushed together.

Constance sashayed in before us, made her way to the table and jumped onto a chair.

As I reached the table, I picked my cat up and moved her to the floor as she meowed in protest.

"This is nice, being able to meet up for breakfast," Suzy said. "It's just like the old days. We should do it more often." She put a hand to her chest. "Even though it's under such sad circumstances."

Mark huffed. "As much as I'm sorry for the dead, I think the choir is going to be a lot more successful, without our departed friend."

"Some of the old members might return," Fred said. "Like Rosemary. I invited her to join us."

As he said it, there was a knock at the door and Tracey answered.

We heard Rosemary before she walked into the lounge bar, she was crying, uncontrollably.

Tracey brought her in with her arm around her shoulder. "There, there, it's been a shock."

Lynn patted the vacant chair beside her. "Hey, Rosemary, lovey. Sit down with me."

"I feel so awful. I was horrible to her and now she's dead." She hiccupped another sob.

Tracey's husband came from around the bar with a glass in his hand. "Get that down you, love," he said as he passed her a brandy.

"Thanks, Roger," she said between sobs.

Constance jumped up from the floor onto Rosemary's lap.

"She senses when people are sad," I said.

Rosemary stroked the top of Constance's head. Being a volunteer for *Cat Lovers*, she was a huge feline fan, especially of Constance, the face of the charity.

"Rosemary, you weren't as rude as I was," Mark said.

"It's fine to be upset that she has passed," Karen said. "But there's nothing to feel sorry about. I guess when your number's up, it's up." She sighed. "And we've lost a few people over the past year because of her ... ways."

"But I blamed her for me leaving the chorus, I told her she was a pig." Rosemary hiccupped and Lynn urged her to drink the brandy.

"I would have said worse," Mark muttered.

Tracey brought out a couple of breakfasts and placed them in front of Suzy and Mark. "She wasn't a popular woman," she said. "If it wasn't a heart attack, I'd have said someone done her in."

Fred sat back in his seat. "Let's not get carried away here." He looked at me. "Just because Becky was there doesn't mean a killer was involved."

"No," I said with a nervous laugh, but I personally thought it likely that I was having breakfast with a murderer.

"I'm not hungry," Rosemary said as Tracey went out to the kitchen.

Lynn patted her hand. "You're going through a tough time, lovey."

Rosemary took in a deep breath. "I'm so sorry for the outburst. I'm fine, really I am."

Roger dished out another couple of cooked breakfasts.

Tracey put a small plate in front of Rosemary. "Door-step buttered toast, it'll settle the nerves in your stomach."

Constance jumped to the floor as my plate arrived and sat against my legs underneath the table.

"If someone killed her, Deloris would have got what was coming to her," Mark said.

"Let's not be unpleasant," Lynn said looking at me then back at the others with a worried expression.

There must be a reason they dislike Deloris other than her singing, I thought as I decided to plug them for information. "Why was she so hated?"

Suzy shot a glance across the table at Mark who was drinking from a mug of tea, then turned back to me. "It was just her way, it's nonsense to think anyone would kill her."

Tracey returned from the kitchen with more filled plates.

"How did she join the choir in the first place?" I asked.

"I introduced her," Tracey said as she placed the final breakfasts on the table and sat down. "She used to eat here on a regular basis when she first came to town. She told me she was trained at The Royal Academy of Music, that she had sung at The Royal Opera House. So I thought she'd be a great addition to the choir."

Fred sighed. "That first rehearsal she turned up to." He shook his head and pursed his lips. "It was difficult."

"We should have given her an audition, like we used to," Karen said

"It wasn't Tracey's fault, that she lied about her extensive experience," Mark said.

"It was unfortunate that she couldn't sing," Suzy added.

"But at the start she was as nice as pie," Rosemary said.

"I agree," Suzy said. "I took her under my wing and invited her to a couple of my dinner parties." She smiled at me. "You must come to my next supper-at-six."

"Suzy's an amazing cook," Tracey said.

"If you're a lady of leisure you have time to put on that type of thing," Mark said.

Suzy rolled her eyes at him. "We always have a sing song afterwards and Fred plays piano."

"I'm rather average," Fred said. "I only know a few songs that I play for the children at school."

"Are you a music teacher?" I asked.

"He was until he became our headmaster," Karen

said smiling at him. "I work at the school too, as a part-time teaching assistant."

"And I was the handyman, until I got the sack," Mark added.

"Sorry, Mark. We had to make cutbacks," Fred said. "The governors made the final decision."

"I know, mate. No worries, I've had a few jobs come in. Did the first before I came here."

"You'll have a lot of free time now that Deloris is gone," Karen said to Mark. "After all the work she made you do on her garden."

He released a long sigh. "Thank goodness. She was a busy body and a pain in the neck."

"What do you mean by busy body?" I asked.

"Maybe we shouldn't be speaking ill of the dead," Fred said hastily as he reached for the HP Sauce and then thumped the bottom of the bottle as brown sauce splodged onto his sausage.

"I agree," Suzy said. "Let sleeping dogs lie."

I chewed on a mouthful of toast thoughtfully as I watched them, they were very familiar with each other. "You all seem quite close, have you been in the choir for long?" I asked as I dug into my full English.

Fred nodded. "We all went to school together and started the choir when we were in our early twenties."

"It was meant to be a one off," Tracey said with a laugh. "To raise money for the church."

"Apart from me," Karen said. "Most of us went off to university, but I didn't come back until Mother got sick a few years ago."

"It was lovely when you turned up," Tracey said. "And joined in with the choir. The whole gang back together." She smiled warmly at Karen.

Karen smiled back. "It's tough being a carer for Mum, but this bunch from school, keep me sane."

"That's why we didn't leave the choir, when everyone else did," Fred said. "We are the original members and we've always met up."

"Even if it was for a drink!" Tracey said.

Mark lifted his coffee mug. "To lifelong friendship, which never dies. And may no-one come between us."

They raised their cups.

Rosemary sniffed and wiped her eyes with a hankie.

I raised my mug of tea thinking that this lot were as thick as thieves. Getting any information out of them was going to be difficult.

CHAPTER 5

Having been home for ten minutes, there was a thud at my front door. I opened it to find Brad glowering at me.

"Come in. Are you a tea or a coffee?" I said with a smile.

"It's not a social call, James," Brad said. He seemed to refer to everyone by their family name, even his fiancée.

Constance hissed at him. She really was not his greatest fan.

Brad followed me to the kitchen where I switched the kettle on, even though he had refused my offer of refreshments.

Constance gave him a stare with her ears flipped back.

Brad remained in the kitchen doorway, near

filling it, as if he didn't want to come in and sit down. "Tell me what you saw," he said in a gruff voice.

As I spoke to him, I felt a surge of energy in my chest, because I knew in that moment, he had accepted me. Accepted I was psychic, accepted that I was of use and was accepting my help with official police business. Even though he was glowering at me.

I filled him in on the previous evening's events. "All she has said to me directly is 'I want to sing. I just want to sing.' So, I've no idea who the culprit is, but most of the spirits I see have been killed." I paused as I stared at him. Then continued. "Do you think she was murdered?"

"I'm not permitted to divulge that information to you," Brad growled.

"So that's a yes then?" I said. "Otherwise, you wouldn't be here." I poured hot water into my tea pot. "Do you want me to give you the low down on the members of the choir?"

He nodded silently as I motioned for him to join me at the table.

He reluctantly sloped in and sat down.

I pushed my box of ugly cakes across the table. While we waited for the tea to brew, I reached for my laptop and then sat beside him. I brought up the social media page of Branden Bay Choir, which had a fairly recent photograph on it.

I pointed to Fred. "This is Fred, the choir leader and headmaster of Branden Bay Primary School. This is Karen, she also works at the school as a part-time teacher and the rest of her days are spent looking after her elderly mother. This is Mark who is a handyman. This is Suzy who they described as a lady of leisure. She seems to spend an awful lot of money on her appearance and loves giving dinner parties." I pointed to the next member. "This is Rosemary, a member of the ladies society who volunteers at my charity shop. And this is Tracey..."

"The landlady of The Branden Arms," he said. "I know her."

"They all went to school together and started the choir when they were in their early twenties. It seems that choir members have come and gone but they have been there all this time. I'm guessing they're mid-forties. Karen has lived a lot of her life out of town and re-joined the choir when she returned to Branden Bay."

"Do you have an opinion on them?" He stared at me. "A gut feeling?"

"I don't have to be psychic to know that none of them liked Deloris. They made no secret of that. We had a breakfast get-together this morning and it seemed more like a celebration than mourning."

Brad peeled the wrapper from a cinnamon muffin.

"Having said that, no-one stands out as being a killer, there was tension between Deloris and everyone else last night. The woman endlessly repeated that she was a trained opera singer, but her voice was awful. They thought she was a liar. Have you contacted the next of kin?"

"She has a son who lives in Wales, he's motoring over to officially identify her. But keep away from him, and don't talk to anyone at the station."

I got the message loud and clear, while Brad was happy to hear what I had to say, he didn't want anyone else to know. I poured the tea.

"How do you ... feel about this Deloris?" he asked.

I shrugged my shoulders. "She came across as sneaky. Mark called her a busy body. She had a go at me last night, accusing me of being a career caroller and trying to push her off the top spot." I laughed. "At least I won't have to sing with them anymore. I can't see them continuing with the Christmas programme after this."

"Bad singing doesn't seem much of a motive for murder." Brad took a cookie from the tin.

"I agree but after the last local murder involved a psychopath. It sometimes doesn't take much to kill."

"True." Brad lifted his cup to his mouth then stared at the ugly cake tin. For all the grief this man had caused me, I felt a measure of compassion.

"Do you want to take some home for Lucy?" I said. "These are the café rejects. They taste the same but have come out wonky. I bet she's hungry eating for four. When are they due?" I asked chancing my luck but expecting him to tell me to mind my own business.

"A caesarean is booked for the fifth of January. But, James, I want this settled by then. Smith wanted to move here to get away from Bristol as we're well known to the underworld there. Living in a small seaside town is supposed to be the ideal place for a family, but considering the murders here..."

"Well one was a cold case, and to be fair, a few of the murderers have been from out of town. And none were random killings. There aren't any gangs here."

He drained his tea and stood up. "I'm not sure when the post-mortem will be done because of the time of year, but if you hear anything useful, let me know." He passed me his card. "That's my personal mobile, keep this between us, I don't want anyone else thinking this is murder. Not even my team."

Constance sashayed over to him and rubbed up against his leg.

I smiled, Constance was clearly picking up that Brad was suddenly and surprisingly on the same team as us.

"I'll let myself out," he said and walked out of the kitchen.

I followed Brad and watched his car drive away, along Beach Road. I had a big grin on my face. He hadn't said it outright, but Brad was asking me to work with him. I stared at his card as if I'd been given a certificate for good behaviour.

I bent down and picked Constance up. "I think he likes us."

She purred as I walked along my hallway smiling. The café phone rang and I answered it, it was Fred.

"After you left, we discussed the sing-outs and decided that Deloris would have wanted the Christmas shows to go ahead," he said.

I groaned to myself. *Really?* I thought. *Surely not.* And H was coming over for the fair.

"The show must go on," he said. "We're having one last practice tonight, before tomorrow's performance."

"Are you sure?" I said.

"Absolutely. Let's do it for Deloris."

I put the phone down and let out a long sigh. There was no way I could back out of the choir now. H was going to have to watch it as well. I shook my head, he would be ribbing me about it that was for sure. And that would delay Jeff and I setting all the ghost detecting equipment up in the hut, we'd have to wait until after the choir practice."

Jeff came down the stairs. "Did Brad say whether they have found the killer?"

"The official line is that it was natural causes, so no-one is looking for a murderer. Brad was quite clear, we can't tell anyone we suspect that she was killed. He's asked me to keep him updated."

"That's insane. Bad Cop Brad wants you to work for him?"

I laughed. "I doubt he would call it that. More like I'm an informant. I think it's the stress of imminent fatherhood. He doesn't want this hanging unsolved when he's on paternity leave. And anyway, forgetting that, I think I'm going to be haunted by the singing ghost of Deloris and I don't want this to overshadow my Christmas, not with Mum and Dad coming. They don't know anything about the cases, or about my newfound gift. It'll be a shock if they turn up halfway through a murder investigation."

"Brad must be desperate," he said. "He doesn't normally like us getting involved."

I laughed. "I know what you mean."

"Do you need any help?"

"Definitely, I need you by my side on this one."

"Right you are, boss." He beamed at me.

I had a small smile on my face, and felt a little

evil, because what Jeff didn't realise, was that I had decided to recruit him into the choir.

JEFF and I reached the hut at seven o'clock. It took some persuasion once he realised that he had to join in with the choir practice before we could call Deloris' spirit up. But I knew he would say yes as right from when I first discovered my gift in the spring, Lynn had told me that for every 'Bridge Medium' (that's my type apparently) there is a gate-keeper. Someone to look out for them and be their protector. Jeff had overheard and was convinced that it was him. I wasn't so sure myself, but it did work to my advantage. He felt it impossible to refuse when I asked for help.

Lynn greeted us at the door with a tearful Rosemary. "She's agreed to come back and sing," she said.

Rosemary's eyes were red. "I still can't believe she's dead. I feel so awful." She wiped her eyes. "She did say she had heart issues."

I nodded. "She loved to sing." I just hoped her spirit wasn't going to be in full voice again that evening. "If you don't mind," I said looking around the room to catch as many glances as I could. "I've invited my lodger, Jeff to join the choir."

"You're the famous ghost hunter, aren't you?" Karen asked him with a hand to her throat.

"Thanks for standing in," Suzy said. "I've followed your stories in the Gazette. It's nice to have young blood in the fold, Jeffrey," she said breathlessly, smiling at Jeff as she flicked her raven hair off her shoulder. "I can call you Jeffrey, can I?" She asked staring into his eyes. "My first boyfriend was called Jeffrey, such a classic name for someone of your generation."

"I'm named after my mum's brother," Jeff mumbled and appeared to gulp.

"Jeff's a really good boy," Lynn added, emphasising the word *boy*.

"I hope you won't be calling Deloris' spirit up," Tracey said to him.

"Becky only tends to see people who were murdered," Jeff said.

There followed a short silence and I looked around the room as everyone stared at Jeff.

"I'm here because I used to sing in the church choir as a boy," Jeff said.

Suzy smiled. "How amazing, we need a new soloist as Rosemary isn't interested in that now, are you dear?"

Rosemary shook her head and wiped her eyes.

I sucked in my lips to stop a smile from growing over my face. Jeff was difficult to scare, I mean he hunted ghosts for fun, but his face flushed crimson and he stammered without making a coherent sentence. I guessed that he was finding Suzy's attention a little difficult to deal with.

"Maybe I should audition you for the part now?" Fred asked.

"Er, no. I don't like singing on my own," Jeff said.

"I'll cheer you on," Suzy said.

"Down cougar woman. Let's get on with it," Mark said.

Suzy tutted and led Jeffrey into position.

My heart filled as we sang together. Without the harsh tones of Deloris' voice, I have to say, we sounded pretty good and Fred and Suzy added harmonies."

"That was beautiful," Lynn said wiping a tear from her eye.

"They couldn't do harmonies with Deloris here, she put them off," Mark said.

The rest of the practice went well and we bade everyone farewell and arranged to meet them the following evening at the fair by the Christmas tree, at five thirty p.m.

Once the choir members had left, Jeff, Lynn and me collected his paranormal gear from the van and brought it in. He wanted to set his whole rig up with recording equipment. As he shut the van door, he turned to me. “Boss, don’t make me sing at the fair tomorrow night.”

“But you said you were a choir boy.”

“It was part of me being undercover. I’ve never sung in a choir before.”

“We’re hardly under cover,” I said. “And your voice was in tune.”

“I’ve got friends now, up at the D.I.Y. store, I’m known now around town, what are they going to think if they go to the Christmas Fair and see me singing with you lot?”

“I thought you were your own man. Are you bowing to peer pressure?” I asked.

“That Suzy woman keeps hanging onto my arm.” He looked at his feet. “There’s a girl at work I like.”

“Ahh.” I was pleased Jeff was moving on from his ex. “I bet she’ll find you even more interesting if she sees you singing.”

Constance meowed as if in agreement.

I picked her up. “You have a beautiful meow, too,” I said. “A singing cat.”

“Shall we get on with it?” Lynn called from the hut door. “It’s getting late.”

Once inside, I shuddered as Lynn said a protection prayer. Then lifted her arms. “Deloris Noble, please make contact.”

I felt static fill my hands. “She’s coming,” I said. I opened my eyes as I heard her voice, distant at first and saw the vision of her, like a see-through projection.

Constance's fur bushed out and she hissed.

Noel. Noel... I heard Deloris' sing.

"Can you two hear her?" I asked.

"No, lovey. You'll have to take the lead. I can feel her presence, but I'm not seeing or hearing anything."

"Deloris, how did you die?" I called out to the spirit.

The angels did say... she continued to sing.

"Deloris, please speak to me."

She stopped and looked at me, then pointed. *I want to sing. I just want to sing.*

"But I need to know if you were killed."

She belted out the next line. *Was to certain poor shepherds in fields as they lay.*

I turned to Lynn. "She won't answer and said she wants to sing. I don't think she wants me to interrupt." I put my hands on my ears as the singing became louder.

"Deloris, lovey. Please answer Becky. Who killed you?" Lynn called out.

I watched as Deloris carried on singing through the verse until she reached the chorus.

Noel, Noel. Noel...

"I don't think she's going to communicate with us," I said as Constance hissed at my feet.

"It is quite soon, lovey. She only passed yesterday."

"I'll leave the rig up overnight," Jeff said. "The SLS picked up her spirit being."

I sighed as I watched Deloris, I didn't need a rig to pick her up. The volume of her singing was pretty high.

She reached her last note then fizzled out.

I picked Constance up to calm her down. "Let's see how the sing-out goes tomorrow night. We need to get close to the choir members. There are secrets there, I know it and I intend to find out what they are."

CHAPTER 6

The following evening, although I was nervous about the sing-out, I was excited for the Christmas Fair and had butterflies in my stomach at the thought of seeing H. I'd been making cookies in the shape of Christmas trees all day. I'd decorated them with green frosting and multi-coloured fondant balls and tasked Jeff with placing the stars on top at a long table against the side wall of the cafe.

"What's the plan of action tonight?" Jeff said as he stuck another star on a cookie. "And I'm still not happy about it. Everyone's got wind of it and are coming to watch. And Mum will be there too."

"I must say, Jeff — your singing is really good. You won't let them down."

Jeff laughed. "Mum always said I had the voice of

an angel when I was a kid. But, boss, I don't want to sing with that lot."

"Me neither. But we have to keep an eye on them. I was awake all night listening to Deloris' ghost singing on and off. Every time I got to sleep she started up again."

"At least she stays in the hut and isn't in your bedroom. Can't you wear ear plugs?"

I shook my head. "No, I'll hear it in my head and the static keeps me awake, too." I yawned. "I don't want it ruining my Christmas." I looked up as Lynn came into the café from the kitchen, followed by Constance.

"How are we going to move forward with the case?" she asked.

"I'm going to get each of them alone, one at a time. I'm interviewing Mark today. I've asked him to fix the lock on my en-suite bathroom door."

"I didn't know it was broken? I could have fixed it for you," Jeff said.

"It wasn't broken until I pulled it off this morning. I just want an opportunity to interview the guy without the others around."

As if on cue Mark entered the café with a toolbox. Constance sashayed over to him staring up, as if trying to work him out.

. . .

"HOW DID THIS COME OFF?" Mark asked as he bent over and looked at the lock on the door of my en-suite bathroom.

"It got caught on something I was carrying," I said.

Constance meowed as if to say, *you liar.*

"I bought a new lock with me. This won't take long."

"How's business?" I asked casually.

"I've picked up a few clients, but not enough to cover the salary I used to earn up at the school. Until they laid me off."

"Why was that?"

"They're going to use contractors. Rather than have someone permanently on site."

"It's all about cutting costs these days, I guess."

He nodded. "It's not going to keep my bills paid or the wife off my back."

"And with Deloris gone, you won't get any money for doing her garden."

"Huh, she never paid me a bean."

"She didn't seem to be popular," I said.

"I've always enjoyed the choir, ever since the early days. You get out of the house and leave your troubles at home – but not this year. It's been a nightmare with that woman involved. The choir was much better before she joined. There was quite a group of us. Twenty-four at one point. A good mix of people and ages, then Deloris rocked up and they all started leaving, one by one. We should've kicked her out from the start. She couldn't even sing."

"What was her background?"

"She said she moved here from Swindon, that she was a widow and had worked and studied in London. But no details other than the constant Royal Academy of Music references."

"Do you think she was there?"

"I doubt it. Her voice was awful. But she thought she was a prima blinking donna."

"I sense she wasn't popular with anyone."

Mark dropped the lock on the tiled bathroom floor.

Constance darted away and jumped on my bed.

Mark sighed as he picked it up. "She started off as nice as pie and then got friendly with you, took you into her confidence then ... wham."

"Yes?"

He shook his head. "Just ignore me, I was thinking aloud." He stood up. "I think we all need to move on and forget all about her, then build up the choir again. By Easter we could be back to a full chorus. Rosemary's already back and we've got you and Jeff as new members."

I didn't want to leave it like that. "Do you think Deloris had something on some members of the choir?"

Constance gave a low meow from the bed.

I felt my heart race, I knew there were definitely secrets to be revealed and that Mark was fobbing me off.

"Look, she was a busybody and manipulative. But as the report online said, she died of a heart attack, so there's nothing here for you to investigate." He raised his eyebrows at me. Clearly realising I was plying him for information. "Now you better stop chatting to me else I'll never get this done. Cup of tea would be nice."

I went back to the café to pick him up a drink and cake, I may not have found much out but I was pretty sure Deloris had been blackmailing someone, maybe someone that saw fit to kill her.

LATER, Jeff, Lynn and me got ready in our singing outfits of black trousers and Christmas jumpers. Luckily Jeff had a full supply of jumpers at his mother's house, which he'd picked up for us. His mother liked to buy him a festive jumper every year. To be fair, mine was so big on me, it looked more like a dress. It had a Christmas tree on it and I put hair ties around the cuffs, and puffed out the sleeves, otherwise they would have hung down to my knees. But it looked quite good. Jeff had a jumper with Rudolf and Lynn wore one with a snowman.

As we walked along the prom pushing the cookie cart, the air was bitter.

"It's okay for you Constance," I said to my cat. The last time I had brought her over to the prom she went missing, so I put her inside a pet carrier and perched it on the end of the cart.

She hissed at me, she really didn't appreciate it and I decided to hand her over to H as soon as I saw him. I tried to calm her down, promising extra salmon. As I spoke, my breath was visible in the cool air and I pulled my coat towards me. It certainly was a chilly evening, but the skies were clear and that was a blessing — having to sing in the rain would have been awful.

We reached the funfair to find the market stalls all set up. I stopped and scanned the place. In the summer months it was a hive of activity with the *Coconut Shy*, *Catch a Duck*, *Hook a Ring on the Stick*. But it had been changed to Christmas themed stalls, including a *Christmas Pudding Shy*, *Catch a Snowman* and *Hook a Ring on the Candy Cane*. Multicoloured fairy lights lined the tops of all the stalls. The Christmas Fair always ran the day before Christmas Eve and provided late night shopping with many local traders bringing their wares for sale. People came in from surrounding towns and villages, bringing their children to see Santa. Couples came for the mulled wine, and it was seen as a romantic event.

With romance in mind, I scanned the area to see if I could find H, he said he would meet me here, but timing was never exact when coming up the motorway. Part of me hoped he would be late and miss the singing.

"It looks amazing," Lynn said as we walked through the market.

Annie waved at us and came over. "The choir's going to be so special with the three of you singing."

"Don't get too excited," I said.

"I'm not happy," Jeff muttered leaning on the cart.

"We've got to sell the cookies first," I said. "We've half an hour before our warmup."

"Hey isn't that Mark?" Lynn said pointing ahead.

I squinted, yes it was Mark and he was talking to Suzy. He ran a hand through his hair as we approached them.

"Hi there," I said.

"Jeffrey, have you been practicing?" Suzy said with a grin.

Jeff blushed and Mark slipped away.

"Can I have a few of those to take home?" She pointed to the cookies.

"Of course," I said as I handed over a pack. "Jeff helped to decorate them."

She poked him in the chest, right on Rudolf's nose. "A man of hidden talents, aren't you, Jeffrey."

Jeff remained silent.

"That'll be five pounds," I said with a smile. "The proceeds are going to the donkeys."

"How nice," she said as she took the packet and paid.

"I need to interview Suzy as soon as possible," I said to Jeff as she walked away. "She was clearly discussing something with Mark, he was probably telling her that we're on the case. I'm going to need you with me to butter her up."

Before Jeff had a chance to protest, Karen approached us. "You've been busy," she said as she looked at the cookies. "And it's so sweet of you donating to the fund. Deloris loved the donkeys."

Fred came over rubbing his hands together. "Let's get warmed up. Mark has set up the music."

We walked towards the Christmas tree, which was not yet lit.

Tracey was chatting away to Mark and Karen was sliding a C.D. into the music player hooked up to the P.A. system.

"Glad you could make it," Tracey said to me.

"So, what was the real deal with Deloris?" I asked

her. “Everyone hated her but you all let her stay in the choir. Why?”

“Fred wasn’t hard enough to kick her out. If he had, at the start, we would be much stronger and have more people.”

“So why didn’t you like her?” I asked.

“She always got her nose in everyone’s business,” she said.

“What exactly?” I asked.

Tracey shook her head. “The sort of private things they don’t want spread around. I’m not about to go into any details.”

Over Tracey’s shoulder, I saw H. I waved at him and he came over.

“You look festive,” he said.

Constance wailed from her cat bag and Tracey moved away.

A warmth carried all over my body. I knew I’d fallen hook line and sinker for the guy who was the epitome of tall-dark-and-handsome. I’d given up being cool and stepped forward for a hug. “I’m so pleased you’re here. Wish me luck.”

He kissed the top of my head.

‘Oh,” I said pointing to the cart. “Could you get Constance out of that pet bag and hold on to her? She’s not happy in there, I should have locked her inside at home. I’m becoming a bit of a nightmare now, taking her everywhere I go.”

"Ok. I'll mind her." He kissed me again then stepped back. "Break a leg."

I laughed. "Knowing me, I will."

He fished Constance out of her bag.

"I wish you were at mine for dinner this year," I said.

"There'll be other years, I'm sure," he said as he held a purring Constance and stroked her head.

"Come on you two love birds, Becky has to perform," Annie said with a laugh.

We moved towards the Christmas tree and Suzy sidled up to Jeff. "It's chilly, let's all huddle up together."

Jeff looked as if he was warming up, as his face flushed red.

As we started with a scale, a crowd began to form next to the tree with Jeff's mum right at the front. She even gave me a little wave, she had warmed up to me in recent months.

Andrew Farr, the owner of the fair spoke into a megaphone. "Can we all have silence please for the Branden Bay Choir."

I smiled as we spread out facing the crowd in our agreed formation. Well, when I say spread out, Suzy was still clinging onto Jeff's arm. And I noticed his mother scowling at her from the crowd.

As we began, I remembered what it was like to

perform. A growing excitement bubbled to the top. Then it was obliterated by a buzz of static.

Oh no, I thought as I saw Deloris' spirit float over and hover beside me. I put my hand to my ear as her spirit breath blew across my face while she sang. I could not hear my own voice. But I could just about make out Constance wailing from H's arms. I gave Fred an apologetic glance and looked back at my song sheet, trying to concentrate as the static fizzed over my body. I looked to H and Annie who gave me smiles of encouragement, as Deloris belted the notes out. I struggled through the performance.

At the end of the five songs, Andrew Farr reached for his megaphone. "Gather around everyone, the Christmas tree lights are about to be switched on. And I have the pleasure of having a local celebrity here, to do the honours." He beamed at me. "Becky James."

Annie cheered and the audience followed with applause.

I groaned. "You didn't warn me about this?" I said to Andrew.

He handed me the megaphone. "Just say a few words."

I shook my head at him as he passed the horn shaped gadget to me. I took a deep breath. "Firstly, I would like to play tribute to our choir member,

Deloris Noble who sadly passed away two nights ago."

The crowd hushed. Deloris had fizzled out, but I still felt pins and needles in my hands.

"I didn't know her well, but I do know how much she loved to sing."

The crowd gave a long clap.

Andrew handed me the controller to switch on the lights.

"May Branden Bay have a happy Christmas with family," I said then switched them on. They flickered, as a burst of static went through my arm.

Andrew looked concerned, but they settled down as I passed the controller back to him.

I stepped back as I looked at the tree. Andrew Farr did not do things by halves. It looked amazing with multicoloured lights, there must have been thousands of them as the tree twinkled, it's star so high up, the backdrop of the clear night sky made it appear as if it belonged there. When the applause subsided, people looked at the tree and whispered as they pointed out their favourite decoration.

After the crowd dispersed, H took my hand and we walked around the market. Taking it in turns to carry Constance. I bought quite a few decorations for my own tree.

We had a mulled wine, and some sausage rolls. I

didn't eat any mince pies, I'd gone off mince pie as I associated it with Deloris.

We watched Jeff play pin-the-tail-on-Rudolf and sniggered as we saw his mother hit Suzy with her handbag when she tried to drag him off to the mistletoe.

"Are you coming back to mine?" I asked H.

He nodded and took my hand.

As we walked towards my house, he looked down at me. "You can tell me all about this death, which I'm guessing you think was murder. I might be out of town but I still keep tabs on what's going on."

"I'd rather not," I said. "I just want to focus on us."

He squeezed my hand as we chatted and laughed on our way back to mine.

CHAPTER 7

I waved H off in the morning, Constance sat on the wall with the breeze ruffling her fur. I breathed in the fresh wintry sea air. Even though there was likely to be a killer at large in Branden Bay, I had a smile on my face, because it was Christmas Eve and my parents were returning home. I looked forward to introducing them to H, although that would not be until after Christmas Day. But I expected my parents would stay for some time.

I'd asked H to try and get out of Christmas working but with him being the newest person on the team at Exeter police station, he had been bottom of the list on the Christmas rota. The fact that he was leaving Exeter in the new year didn't earn him any favours either.

I picked Constance up and turned back to the house, I had no time for delays, I had so much to do, not forgetting the fact that I wanted to find out who killed Deloris.

Once inside, Lynn came into the café from the rear entrance. "I'm ready and raring to go. Are you expecting many in the café today?"

"Maybe. The sun's out and a lot of people will be ready for Christmas by now." I reached for my phone. "I'm calling Karen. I want to interview her first."

"Don't you think you should leave it until after Christmas, lovey?"

I shook my head. "Not with my parents coming. I was kept awake again last night."

Lynn raised her eyebrows. "So H stayed over did he?"

"Lynn, that was not the reason I could not sleep. And for your information, he slept in the spare room."

Lynn winked at me. "Of course, lovey."

"It was Deloris and her singing that kept me awake. I have to find her killer."

"So why are you starting with Karen, is she your prime suspect?" Lynn asked

"Karen's quiet. I guess she probably spends a lot of time watching the others," I said.

Lynn turned on the coffee machine. "What are you going to do? Ask her to test your Christmas cake?"

"No. I'm calling her on the pretence that I need someone to help me with my spreadsheets."

Annie arrived for her morning coffee and I went out the back to make the call to Karen in private.

AS SOON AS KAREN ARRIVED, I took her into my snug. It was a small living room at the back of my house which looked out to the garden. In the summer the sun pooled in and Constance loved to sit in there, but in the winter it was often quite chilly.

On the coffee table, I had set out a pot of tea with two cups, a milk jug and a sugar bowl. A freshly baked stollen sat on a board. I dished out the drinks and cake.

I took a bite of the powdery sugar dusted cake, which had a line of marzipan running through the centre. I'm not too modest to say, it tasted divine. I'd been given the recipe by Rosemary who was taught how to bake it during a Ladies' Society demonstration.

"So here it is," I said after wiping my hands on a festive paper napkin. I passed her my laptop. "I need to record this week's earnings and I can open this spreadsheet, but it won't let me make any changes. Lynn is clueless when it comes to computers and Jeff's at work. I'm one of those people that like to be organised and want all the takings up to date." I thought I sounded convincing.

Karen looked at the screen. "You have to enable editing. It looks like Dannie has protected the sheet, to ensure it's not updated by mistake."

"Ahh," I said. "You learn something new every day."

"You just click this button here." Karen pointed the mouse at the correct button.

"That was quick," I said. 'Thanks ever so much. Can you stay for another slice of stollen? I have plenty here."

"Yes, please," she said smiling. One thing I could do was woo people with cake.

"So," I said. "What did you really think of Deloris? The others didn't seem to like her much." I took another bite of cake.

Karen shook her head. "The woman was a troublemaker."

"I saw you speaking to her, at the last rehearsal she attended."

"I was trying to convince her to forget the solo as I felt it was unfair. I said that she was yet to build a rapport with Fred, which was essential for a duet. I felt she was bulldozing him into it and he was clearly too polite to refuse."

Hmmm, I thought. *Maybe not polite, maybe he was being forced.*

"Did Deloris get along with Fred?"

"Not really," Karen said. "But then I have yet to meet someone who did get along with her."

"Was she well off?" I asked.

"Yes, she was a widow and lived off investments. Property, shares and the like. She said her departed husband was extremely well off. She never spoke of her career, only of The Royal Academy of Music, but she always had money."

"Do you think she had something on Fred and that's why he let her do the duet?"

"Well…"

"Yes?"

"I shouldn't really say but Fred got Mark the sack from the school. I overheard Deloris say she was going to tell Mark it was his doing, rather than the Governors, unless Fred let her sing the solo."

"Are you saying she blackmailed him?"

"That's quite a strong word. Let's say she was persuasive."

I had to remind myself, that as far as local news was concerned, there was no murder, Deloris had died of natural causes, albeit after eating one of my mince pies.

"So," she asked in a low voice. "Have you or Lynn seen her spirit? Is that why you're asking questions because you think she was..." She paused and visibly gulped. "Killed?"

"I, erm. I don't know if Lynn has," I said. I didn't want to lie, and I was thankfully saved by Constance who was outside, meowing and scratching at the glass, to be let inside. Clearly too lazy to go through the cat flap in the kitchen. I stood up and opened the door. I'd established what I needed from Karen, I didn't now want to be answering her questions and it was plain to see from what Karen had said, Deloris was not only a busybody, she was a blackmailer.

After seeing Karen out, my phone rang with a video call from my parents.

"Hi, Mum, Dad," I said, feeling excited.

"Are you okay?" Dad asked. "You look tired."

"Yes, everything's fine," I said, not mentioning anything about singing spirits keeping me awake at night. After all, how could I now tell them that I had been involved in five murder investigations and had just stumbled on yet another body? I was leaving it until they arrived home, to explain what had happened to me, and that I had this gift for seeing the dead. I wanted to tell them in person.

"We need to go Christmas shopping and have to buy some warm clothes," Mother said. "We only have our summer wardrobe with us. I'll let you know when we leave Exeter, but it might be some time before we arrive as the roads will be busy with everyone driving home for Christmas."

"I'm singing tonight up at Branden Bay Church for their Carols by Candlelight. Have you still got your key?"

"Yes," Dad said.

"Great," I said. "If I'm not here, let yourselves in and then if you're up for it, the service is at six thirty."

Dad frowned at the screen. "Don't overdo it. I'll feel happier when I get home and give my little girl a hug."

After saying our goodbyes, I ended the call. I had to get this case solved and quick.

Lynn came in. "I've got a few customers in. What time shall I close?"

"Shut at three as you'll want to freshen up. I'm leaving here at half five. It's going to be fab."

"I do hope that none of the choir are killers. The thing that worries me, is that everyone seems an awfully lot brighter than they have been for months. It's as if they're relieved Deloris has gone."

"Just because they're relieved, doesn't mean they killed her," I said.

"Suzy's come alive." She looked at Jeff as he walked into the snug having finished his early shift. "But that might be something to do with our Jeff."

I laughed and Constance meowed.

"What's the big joke?" he asked.

"Nothing, we were just saying how the choir members seem happier since Deloris died."

My phone dinged with a text and I read it. "Brad's coming over." I looked up at them wide eyed.

"I'll get back to the café, lovey." Lynn hurried away.

"I've got my assignment to do," Jeff said as he turned and left the room.

It wasn't just me that was a little bit scared of Bad Cop Brad.

BRAD FROWNED when Lynn showed him into my snug.

He walked over to the window and looked out to the garden. "I've left Smith with her mother," he said.

Constance wound herself around his legs, but he paid no attention to her. Considering she had once taken a chunk out of his ankle I had to admit, Brad was one hard cop.

"The midwife is coming over for a home visit as the contractions have started." He turned around to face me with a grave expression. "They're coming."

I just managed to stop myself from laughing and covered it with a smiling cough. He had referred to his babies as if the enemy were just about to burst over the hills and invade the town.

"When she's admitted, I'll be spending most of my time at the hospital. I've come to give you an update. It was definitely a heart attack that killed Deloris Noble. Her medical records showed that she had been told repeatedly to adopt a healthy lifestyle, as a heart attack was on the cards without it."

"But?" I asked, sensing there was more.

"There were signs of a fall, and the mince pie in the mouth was not the natural way a person would eat their food. It could be considered manslaughter if someone stuffed it into her face and pushed her over, bringing on an early death."

"I see."

Constance continued to rub up against his legs.

"They've sent your mince pie off for testing and requested a toxicology report with samples collected through the post-mortem, in case a poison was administered that induced the heart attack. That of course, would also indicate murder."

"Is there any way you can let me have access to Deloris' house?" I asked. Time was running out if Brad was soon to be on paternity leave. "Having met the choir and interviewed a couple of them, I'm convinced Deloris was a blackmailer, but they're all keeping tight lipped. If I find out what the secrets are, it should hopefully lead me to the killer."

Brad ran a hand across his closely shaven head. "I'll be unable to obtain a warrant without a crime."

"I know it's not the correct procedure, but we don't have much time."

I was sure I could hear Brad growl as he considered what I was saying.

"It'll do us both a favour," I said.

"I have a key, obtained from the victim's bag." Brad checked the time on his phone. "I'm supposed to be signing off before my…" He paused and I saw him visibly swallow. "Paternity leave. But no telling anyone that I'm taking you to the house, especially not that reporter friend of yours."

I shook my head vigorously. "Izzy's away in London. And Lynn and Jeff know not to repeat anything."

Once outside, I got into Brad's car leaving a protesting Constance back at the café with Lynn. I was in the front passenger seat. I'd been in his car before, but only in the back after he'd arrested me.

He drove us along Beach Road. "Smith wanted to live by the seaside, thinking it would be great for the kids to grow up here. I've given up a career in Bristol to run the show here and all I see is death."

"The beach is nice though," I said in a cheery voice. "And the local school gets good reports."

"Shame the headmaster is a murder suspect."

"You have a point," I said and decided my

attempts to make the town sound nice, were not working.

After picking the keys up from the police station, Brad drew up outside Deloris' house.

"Wow," I said. "This is a nice property."

He pulled a bunch of keys from his pocket. "See if you pick anything up. I've heard of colleagues using psychics before, but it's always off the record and none of them are as much of a pain as you."

"Charming," I said as I took the keys.

"Be quick." His phone dinged with a text and he made a call immediately, presumably to Lucy.

I entered the house, unnoticed. Once inside I saw that it had a lovely hall with sage green walls, deep skirting boards and a dado rail, both picked out in white gloss. Wooden flooring ran from the hall into each room. The house was neat and well-kept. I decided to go upstairs first.

As I climbed the stairs, I stopped to look at the display of pictures depicting theatre stages with shows in progress. I frowned at one of the photographs, it was of a beautiful young woman, with blonde ringlets singing her heart out. It looked like Deloris, but I thought it unlikely to be her, considering her substandard vocal skills. *Maybe it was a relative?* I thought.

Once on the landing, I found an office. Again, it appeared freshly decorated and was tidy. Deloris had much better taste in interior décor than she did in clothes. Her red dress with the snowmen on it came to mind. I opened the drawers of the desk, wearing gloves which Brad had given me. It was not locked. After rummaging inside, I could not locate any bank statements. I presumed Deloris used online banking. It looked as if Brad would have to wait until the bank responded to any police enquiries. However, I found a folder with 'Choir' written on it and pulled it out. Opening it up, I saw a leaflet from an organisation called 'Elixir of Life', with the tagline *A New You.* I frowned, it looked like a plastic surgery type establishment. Deloris didn't look as if she'd had any work done herself.

I flicked through the folder and came to a printout of a newspaper article, reporting on stolen silverware from Branden Bay Church in the 1990's. I scanned the article and wondered whether it had ever been found. I continued to look through the folder and found a picture of a man embracing someone. I squinted and brought it closer to my eyes, not being able to identify the people, as it was too grainy. Finally, there was a letter from the Branden Bay Donkey Sanctuary acknowledging receipt of a £100 donation.

I smiled as I went down the stairs and felt I need not look any further around the house. I had concrete clues here and appreciated that it was so much easier conducting an investigation with the police on side. And easier was what I needed if I was to solve this by teatime.

As I came out of the house with the folder, Brad was talking on his mobile as he sat in the driver's seat of his car. A woman walked up the path of the neighbouring property.

"You're that investigator, aren't you?" the woman asked.

I shot a glance at Brad. This probably wasn't good. I looked back at the woman, I vaguely recognised her and had seen her in the café a few times.

I nodded at her, there was no point denying it.

"Are you investigating Deloris' death?" Her eyes widened. "Was it murder?"

I smiled. "No, I sang with her in the choir. I'm just picking this folder up, which we need for Carols by Candlelight this evening." I flashed her the folder with 'Choir' written on the front.

"Thank goodness," the neighbour said. "Poor Deloris. She loved that choir, and they were always around here."

"I didn't know they practiced with her?"

"Oh no, not for a practice, they came around individually. She was so well loved and had so many friends."

"Like who?" I asked wondering how the neighbour could have got it so wrong.

"The headmaster came a few times, always bringing her fresh flowers and did her shopping for her. And the guy who used to do her gardening, what's his name, Mark he did so much. Built a patio and a shed. That Tracey from the pub popped over a couple of times with bottles of drink and then of course Karen was often over here. I think she did her cleaning. I know her from the school as my grandchildren go there and have her as a teacher. And not forgetting her mate Suzy, she was always telling me about her fabulous supper parties. They had a whale of a time. Deloris was so loved, and she was such a great listener." She put the key in the lock in her front door.

So she must have had something on all of them, I thought as I watched the neighbour go inside her house. If they detested her, why would they be bending over backwards for the woman. But one thing I was certain of, none of them had loved Deloris. The question I had to answer was – who hated her enough to kill?

I got into Brad's car and handed him back the set of keys.

"Did you see anything supernatural?"

I shook my head. "But she was blackmailing them all. I found this folder with details in. Can I take it back to mine?"

Brad took it from me and looked inside. "I'll

collect it when you're finished with it. Do you have a safe?"

"Yes."

"Keep it in there. I don't want it to go missing. I'll be in touch, but it might not be for some time. Lucy's on her way to the hospital with her mother, the contractions have stopped but they want to keep her in."

It was the first time I'd ever heard Brad call his fiancée by her first name.

"Do you know anything about stolen silverware from Branden Bay Church in the nineties?"

"As you know, I'm new to the area, in the 90's I was undercover witnessing drug deals, not checking for missing cutlery from a church," he said wistfully as if he missed the early days of his career. He started the car engine. "I'll ask Wright to check the database and will pass you the details." He drove away from the house.

"I've got six suspects. I'll try and whittle it down for you today."

"If you get anything, call. If I don't answer, leave a message and I'll get back as soon as I can."

"I'll text you the login details for my cat's G.P.S. collar. I usually have her with me, so you'll know where I am. And there's a computer in Deloris' office that you might want to get one of your forensics team to log into."

He nodded. "I'll ask Wright to collect that, if there is any indication of murder either from the toxicology report, or from you."

"All the signs that she was a blackmailer are there, all I need to do is match the evidence in this folder to the right suspects."

CHAPTER 8

I asked Brad to drop me at the High Street and I went straight to the pop-up Christmas shop and bought a set of very nice sparkly Christmas hats. I decided to use them as an excuse to visit every member of the choir before Carols by Candlelight. And Rosemary was first. I passed my favourite restaurant, Corelli's, and smiled. Myself and H had eaten there many times. I literally couldn't wait for him to move back to Branden Bay so that we could have a proper relationship and not the long-distanced kind.

I soon reached the Cat Lovers charity shop and once inside, I was pleased to see a few customers there. Connor, my partner in the charity shop was convalescing on Grand Canaria, following an injury he had sustained. He was spending Christmas there with his family and friends. But before he left, he had managed to recruit half of Branden Bay Ladies' Society with his charm, to help out in the shop. I had taken him to speak at one of their meetings about my previous case. And they were pretty much running it for us, which was a relief, I had enough on my plate. Constance and me, were the faces of the charity and there was a rather off-putting life-sized cardboard cut-out of us in the front window.

A couple of the customers pointed at me and whispered, looking at my full tote bag which had the evidence folder and hats inside.

"I left Constance at home," I said to them with a smile.

'Hi, darling," Rosemary said having finished serving a customer. "Are you looking forward to the church service tonight?"

I smiled. "Yes, I'm hoping my parents will be there. I've bought us all some fancy headwear." I reached into my bag and pulled out a sparkly hat and passed it to her.

"Very swish," she said. "Thank you, it's a great idea."

"All I need now is a sparkly Christmas collar for Constance." I looked through the display which was next to the checkout. "Ah, this one," I said, having found a glittery green and red collar. I reached into my pocket for a five-pound note and handed it over. "It's sad Deloris has gone, even if you didn't get along with her."

Rosemary's chin trembled.

I felt instantly awful. "Hey, I wasn't being judgemental. Not many people seemed to like her, even though it appears they bent over backwards for her. At least you were honest about it."

Rosemary nodded but said nothing. I suspected she was about to cry. So, I said goodbye and told her that I would see her later at the church, feeling a little more than guilty as I left the shop and saw her reach for a hankie.

As I stepped into the street, I spotted Jeff and called him over.

"Hey, what are you up to?" he asked.

"I've been up to Deloris' house." I lifted the folder part of the way out of my tote bag. "I've collected solid clues that indicate blackmail. I'm visiting all of the suspects on the pretence that I'm providing them each with a sparkly hat and will interview them. I bought a hat for you too."

"Great," Jeff said unconvincingly.

"Will you come with me?" I asked. "I'm going to pick Constance up first. Brad's tracking me via her collar."

"Of course," he said with a grin.

"You'll come in useful when we visit Suzy."

Jeff sighed. “That woman scares me. Who are we visiting first?”

“Karen, I saw her earlier, she’s the quiet one and I get the feeling she has a lot more to say than she’s letting on.”

I’d already got a list from Lynn of the addresses for all the suspects. The choir used to circulate contact details of all members. I could see from the list that the choir had indeed shrunk in size from over twenty people.

Once we had picked Constance up, I collected another tote bag and Constance jumped inside.

We reached Karen’s house and knocked on her door. “We need to get these people on side,” I whispered. “So let’s be really nice.”

The door opened. Karen seemed surprised to see us. “Is everything okay?”

I smiled and held up a hat. “We come bearing gifts. I bought us all a hat for the sing-out tonight.”

Her expression softened. “That’s a lovely idea.”

“Can we come in?” I asked. “It’s a bit chilly out here.”

I felt a little nervous as we walked into her dark hall. It was rather creepy with peeling wallpaper.

“I’ve yet to decorate,” she said. “It’s a bit gloomy. But mother doesn’t like change. She’s in the living room in front of the television. Come to my kitchen and morning room. Let's not disturb her – she's become quite fierce in her old age."

I walked along the corridor to the kitchen and heard the television blaring out as I passed the lounge door. "Have you lived here long?"

"Only since Father passed away, five years ago. I've been caring for Mum ever since." She turned around and spoke in a low voice. "She's quite a handful."

"I'm sorry to hear that," I said.

Karen nodded and appeared to swallow. "Coffee or tea?" she asked.

"No thank you, we won't stay long as we need to deliver the rest of the hats," I said.

Karen placed her hand on her kitchen table and leaned forward to face us. "It's no secret around town that you two are private investigators. So, I'm assuming you think Deloris was murdered?" She peered at Jeff and then back at me.

Constance poked her head out of the bag and hissed.

I pushed her head down, deciding to be non-committal. "The police say it was natural causes. And I can't believe that anyone in the choir would kill Deloris — they're all so nice."

She paused as if she was going to say something, then looked out of the back window to her small garden. I sensed that Karen had information I needed.

"Do you think any of them could kill?" Jeff asked gently.

Constance hissed again from my bag.

"None of them liked Deloris." She looked at me. "But murder? It's a bit extreme."

"Did you like her?" Jeff asked.

"She was devious. And so nosey. When I first joined the choir, she wanted to be my best friend. We went for dinner. She invited me over to her place. Asked me all sorts of personal questions. It was like being interrogated. I found her a bit much after a while and then assumed she found me boring because she ditched me. But ..."

"But you realised she might be looking for dirt on you," I said.

"Is that what you think? That she's been silenced?" Karen stood up straight and rubbed the front of her neck.

I nodded. "The mince pie in her mouth was a bit odd. Like it was stuffed in there. Have you heard any gossip?"

"Well..." Karen picked up a tea towel from the table.

"A woman has died, Karen. If there is something you're holding back, we need to know," Jeff said.

Karen looked down. "I think Deloris was a blackmailer." Karen twisted the tea towel in her hands. "But I don't know any secrets other than Fred being responsible for Mark's sacking."

"As the treasurer, and in charge of collecting funds for the donkey sanctuary, is there anything Deloris was blackmailing you for?" I asked this because when we had been rehearsing, I was told the donation to the sanctuary was £1,000 but the receipt I had in the folder was for only £100.

Karen's eyes welled up with tears. "So you've found out then?" She turned away from us. "I was short of cash." She spun around. "Please don't tell anyone, I've been paying the money back. I have the receipts, it'll be settled by the end of January."

I took a deep breath, but remained silent watching her ringing her tea towel.

"I didn't kill Deloris," Karen said.

"No-one has said it was murder," Jeff said.

"But she thinks it was," she said staring at me.

I started to feel a little nervous and Jeff moved closer to me, sensing my discomfort. Constance began a low and long meow, as she always did when I felt uncomfortable. While I had found out Karen's secret, I didn't think she'd kill a woman over £900. It just didn't seem enough, especially if she was nearly done with paying it back.

"I won't tell the others," I said. I also decided I wouldn't tell Brad either, unless Karen turned out to be the killer. There was no point in me spreading everyone's secrets. All I needed was to find the secret that lead to the death. "Don't worry about it, Karen." I'd heard enough and we needed to get on and speak to my next suspect.

"Thank you," she said in a quiet voice. "I'll see you out."

As I passed the front room, I heard the television playing again and felt a short shot of static. Constance hissed from my bag and I pushed her head down as I got the feeling she intended to jump out.

"Mother loves the nature programmes," Karen said with a nervous laugh. "She suffers from headaches so sits in the dark."

I thought that turning the volume of the T.V. down would help with the headache but didn't comment.

Karen opened the lounge door. "I'll come and see you in a minute, Mum."

I saw her mother from the back, sitting in an armchair and thought of my parents, having just travelled around the world. I was looking forward to seeing them, I had not yet received a text to say that they'd left Exeter.

We said goodbye to Karen and she thanked us for the hat before closing the door.

"What do you think, boss?" Jeff asked.

"Not a big enough motive. Next we've got Fred, he's only in the next street."

We were soon on his doorstep and I rang the bell and looked down at my bag as Constance meowed up at me. "Behave yourself, Connie Cat."

The door opened.

Fred was smiling, but it seemed to fade when he saw it was us. "Is there anything wrong?"

"No, we just wanted to give you this." I handed over a sparkly hat. "I thought it would be a nice idea for us to sing tonight with festive headgear."

He lifted the hat up with two fingers and turned his nose up at it. I guess it wasn't his style.

"Everyone else likes them," Jeff said. "I've got one too."

"Of course, yes. Thank you." He nodded at us and began to close the door.

"We just wanted to ask you a couple of questions about Deloris," I called before he totally shut it on us.

Once he had reopened the door, he shook his head. "I have no time for this. You do realise, we only have two hours before the sing-out?"

"I gather Deloris was blackmailing you?" I had no time for politeness.

I saw his eyebrow twitch. He remained silent.

"About you giving Mark the sack and it not being the governors' decision."

He appeared to relax slightly, but still looked annoyed. "Yes, she was putting pressure on me. And I hope that you are not going to follow in her footsteps and threaten to tell Mark."

"Of course not," Jeff said.

"We just want to know, if you think anyone would have motive to kill Deloris."

"Look, children." He stared at me and then at Jeff. "Stop making trouble. Not every death in Branden Bay is a murder." He tutted then slammed the door.

Constance gave an angry meow.

"That told us," Jeff said as we stepped off the doorstep.

"Next we have Suzy," I said.

Jeff grumbled the whole way to her house.

When we arrived, Tracey was coming out and she stopped to stroke Constance.

"Jeffrey, do come in." Suzy beckoned Jeff, and he passed us towards the door.

"Hi," I said to Tracey as she scratched Constance's head. "I'm glad I caught you, I bought everyone a festive hat for the carol service."

"Ooh," Tracey said. "I do love a bit of sparkle. I'm on my way to Mark's if you want me to drop one to him?"

"Can I ask you a question about Mark?"

"Ok." She looked a bit nervous.

"It appears that he has a secret that Deloris was blackmailing him over. She got him to overhaul her whole garden for free."

"Look, Deloris was a busy body, she made up lies." She put her hand out. "I'll give him the hat."

I hesitated, bringing to mind the grainy photograph I'd seen. "I want to hand deliver it myself."

"I'll let him know you'll be over," she said in a clipped tone and turned away.

Constance gave a sorrowful meow.

I watched Tracey walk down the path. I doubted that Deloris was blackmailing anyone with an untruth. *Is it possible that Mark and Tracey are having an affair?* I asked myself.

I walked up the path and knocked on Suzy's door, which she had closed behind her and Jeff.

She answered. "Come in, Becky. Sorry to shut you out, but it's freezing."

I went in and she closed the door behind me. Her hall was decorated with a busy wallpaper.

"I bought you this for the sing-out tonight." I handed her a hat.

"So Jeffrey said. How sweet. I'm looking forward to it."

I looked over her shoulder to see Jeff sitting at her kitchen table, with fear in his eyes.

"Look," I said to Suzy. "Tell me to mind my own business, but was Deloris blackmailing you about anything?" Suzy touched her hairline and the leaflet from the plastic surgery clinic came to mind.

She puffed out. "If you must know, the woman was evil. It seems she was blackmailing a few of us. Not necessarily for money, but for favours. She was blackmailing Fred so he would let her sing the duet and solo and she had the lot of us doing favours. The woman was deranged, thinking she could sing. She must have got herself so worked up about it, she caused her own heart attack. This is why we're not so sad that she passed. Please don't tell me you think she was killed?"

"It was a heart attack, as you said." I didn't add that both myself and Brad had our suspicions that there was more to it. "I was just interested to know why you all seem so pleased she's gone. What were the secrets?"

"No-one in this world has gone through life without doing things they wish to keep private. Deloris was the sort of woman that took you into her confidence and was very good at it. She probably would have done the same to you if she wasn't so threatened. Just accept that justice has been done. And don't interfere."

Constance hissed and Suzy rolled her eyes at her. "Do you ever leave that thing at home?"

Constance's paw shot out of my bag and I

managed to intercept it before she gave a skin busting swipe to Suzy's pale skin.

"Really!" She flicked hair. "Look, It'll be awful for us if this whole nasty business gets blown out of proportion. People around here love to gossip. I don't want our dirty laundry out on show. Please, have some respect."

"Have you had plastic surgery?" I asked outright. Okay, so it was blunt but I was running out of time.

"Who told you that?" she asked, taking a step backwards with her hand to her chest. I'd clearly hit a nerve. "I've only had a little freshening up! Just forget this, Becky. You're making our neighbourhood into some sort of death town and it's really not good for the tourist trade."

I realised I'd outstayed my welcome. Again, I was convinced Deloris had been blackmailing Suzy with the details of what was possibly, extensive surgery. Suzy did have a lack of wrinkles for someone of her age. But again, it was no reason to kill her.

"I'm just dishing Jeffrey up a stew," she said.

I looked through to the kitchen. "It smells tasty."

Jeff mouthed at me. "Help."

"There isn't enough for you, I'm afraid. No doubt you have more to distribute. I won't keep you. Or your moggy." She gestured towards the front door.

I clutched Constance to prevent an attack.

I found myself out on the street and messaged

Jeff to tell him that I was off to Mark's house. I realised that if I was quick enough, I might get to see Tracey again.

I panted as I arrived, I could hear his family before I saw them.

A woman answered the door. "Just pipe down, Josh," she shouted behind her then faced me. "Don't ever have kids. You're that Becky James, aren't you? I love your baking. Well ... I did until I heard about the killer mince pie."

"It wasn't my cooking — Deloris had a heart attack."

"I know, love, I know. I'm just trying to be funny. When you live in a house with six males, you have to make jokes for your own sanity. Even the pet tortoise is a boy. Come in, Mark's expecting you. He's been mighty popular today."

I looked around the house, which was cluttered with toys and heard the sound of screams filling the house. But they weren't screams of death, the children were having fun. This was a happy home. My heart felt heavy, what if Mark was the killer? Would I be breaking up this family? And no wonder he was stressed about losing his job, the poor man had tonnes of responsibility. And Deloris was out of line, blackmailing him over a minor indiscretion with Tracey. Well, assuming it was minor. That was something I needed to find out.

"He's in the garden with Tracey. It's the only peaceful place around here." She gestured behind her.

I walked through the house, being careful not to trip over the toys on the floor. Constance was laying low in my bag. I didn't blame her, goodness knows what the children would have done if they'd seen her. I reached the back door and opened it then stopped, observing Tracey speaking to Mark, who was running a hand through his hair.

"Hi," I called out.

They both looked up. They were clearly expecting me.

"So, where's this hat Tracey was telling me about?" Mark said as I reached them.

I waved it at him. "Here."

"It's not something I'd usually wear, but I don't want to be the odd one out." He put the green sparkly hat on his head. "Nice, it's warm, too."

"I guess you've come to interrogate us about Deloris?" Tracey said. "We know you're investigating. I presume you've seen her spirit?"

I sighed and sat down.

Constance poked her head nervously out of my bag, presumably checking the coast was clear of children.

"It's like this. I'm haunted by Deloris every night, and her singing is keeping me awake."

"You poor thing," Mark said. "That sounds like a real horror show."

"I need to find out how she died so she can move on to the other side," I said.

"Does anyone want some Quality Street?" Mark's wife called from the back door waving the purple tub of chocolates at us.

"Not for me," I said.

The others declined too.

I waited for the door to close. "Look, I've seen a photo of two people embracing. Was Deloris blackmailing you two over it?"

Mark looked harassed, really harassed.

"Me and Roger had a falling out," Tracey said. "I chatted to Mark about it after choir one night." She gestured to him. "Me and him are like family, I've known him since I was four."

"She's Godmother to two of the kids."

"Three, actually," Tracey said then turned to me. "Mark hugged me because I was in tears. It wasn't anything remotely romantic, but Deloris took a photo with her cheap phone. If it was a better picture, you'd see it was innocent."

"So why not call her out?" I asked.

Tracey shook her head. "She hinted that she would show it to my Roger if I didn't fill her drinks cabinet whenever she ran out."

"Can you imagine how heartbroken my wife

would be if she thought I was unfaithful?" Mark said. All it needs is a small seed to sow doubt, which can ruin a relationship. And I'd hate to hurt Maria, she's my everything. And I'd have to give up my friendship with Tracey, who is like family to me. That's why I did Deloris' garden. I knew she was ill. I thought it would be a short-term thing."

"She's been blackmailing all of the choir," Tracey said. "Everyone knows that, but we don't know what each other's secrets are. And neither do we want to, so we would really appreciate it if you kept this matter to yourself."

I nodded. "I've heard enough secrets now, but none are worth killing the woman over. Although, there has been a mention of stolen silverware. Is that something you know about?"

Tracey and Mark exchanged a look.

Tracey frowned. "Well, yes. That was years ago, it was why we started singing, to raise money for the church to replace what went missing. It's a part of our history, the roots of the choir."

"We've raised thousands over the years," Mark said. "It's only this year we started raising for the donkeys, to keep Deloris quiet.

Tracey stood up. "I'd better get back to the pub. Roger needs a break as he'll be working until the last customer leaves tonight. I'll walk down the hill with you." She pointed to Mark's head. "And you don't have to pay for those hats, you know. You can ask Karen to take the money out of the petty cash and refund you. You've only been in the chorus for five minutes."

Clearly, Tracey wanted to change the subject and whilst I had interviewed all of the suspects, I was no closer to finding out what really happened to Deloris.

CHAPTER 9

After chatting to Tracey about the history of The Branden Arms on our way to the seafront, I arrived home and entered via my private entrance, rather than the café which was now closed. Once I reached the kitchen, I found Jeff was also home.

"I can't believe you left me with her," he said frowning.

Constance jumped out of my tote bag and rubbed herself against his legs

"Sorry, but I didn't have much time. And I needed to see Mark. Did you find out anything from Suzy?" I asked.

"Only that she wants to come on a ghost hunt with me, just me and her. She says I give her the shivers and keeps shimmying at me."

"Sorry, Jeff," I said. "I won't leave you with her again." Suzy really seemed to have taken a shine to him.

We were interrupted by Lynn as she brought Rosemary into the kitchen. "I've cleaned the café. We're going to mine to get ready."

Rosemary looked at my snowman shaped Christmas cake. "I love snowmen, they really make me feel Christmassy. Although that snowman dress Deloris wore, nearly put me off."

I laughed. "I know what you mean. It was rather garish."

"We'll see you two up at the church for half five," Lynn said.

Constance gave a long wail as she stared at Rosemary.

"Don't worry, Constance. I'm not leaving you here," I said. "Considering Brad is tracking us via your collar. And talking of collars, I need to also put the sparkly one on."

Lynn and Deloris left via the back door.

Constance hissed as Jeff held her while I put the festive extra collar on.

I plonked myself on the sofa in the snug. I looked up at Jeff as he leaned on the doorframe. "It's great to sit down. I've been on my feet all day."

My phone dinged with a text. "Great, Mum and Dad are on their way and the roads are clear. They'll meet us up at the church. I can't wait for you to meet them." I smiled at him then picked Constance up. "And you."

My cat purred.

"What did you find out from the others, boss?" Jeff asked.

"This stays between me and you. Don't tell Annie, Lynn or anyone else in this world, as I don't want the details spread around. But I'd like to talk it over with you."

"Sure, go on," he said.

I smiled at Jeff as he sat beside me. It was like my first case, when he was the only person I felt I could confide in. "Deloris was blackmailing Fred because he got Mark the sack from the school. She was blackmailing Mark and Tracey because she took a picture of them embracing. They tell me it was innocent, and I believe them, but they didn't want to cause any stress for their respective spouses. As you know, she was blackmailing Karen because she was strapped for cash and instead of sending £1,000 to the donkey sanctuary Karen only sent £100. But she has been paying it back. Deloris also threatened to spread the news that Suzy has had plastic surgery, which only leaves Rosemary who openly disliked her."

"Which one killed her then?"

I sighed. "None of the reasons I've been given

seem compelling enough. And to stuff a mince pie in her mouth. That has a viscousness about it. And there's one piece of information in the choir folder which I'm not totally sure about." I leaned down and picked up my tote bag with the folder and removed the newspaper article. "It's to do with the stealing of silverware from the church. Tracey said they started the choir to help raise funds for the church after the silver had been stolen."

"So, you think Deloris found out who took it?"

"Maybe. That's a bigger crime than the other reasons she was blackmailing them for. It could involve a prison sentence. And socially, it's not a good look around town to be outed for stealing from the Church."

"What about Karen? We know she's already a thief."

"True, and she left town, went to university, and never came back, until she had to," I said. "Maybe she took it with her. I've an excuse to go back to Karen's house. Tracey told me to claim the cost of the hats from her. Maybe she'll break when I mention the silver." I stood up. "Come on."

"Let's do this," Jeff said.

Constance meowed and jumped into my tote bag.

As we reached Karen's house, I rapped on the door.

She soon opened it. “Is there a problem?” she asked with a frown.

“We were coming to ask if I could claim back the money I spent on the hats? Tracey said it normally comes out of the choir fund.”

“What now? We need to be at the church in half an hour.”

“We were passing,” Jeff said.

“You’d better come in then.” She stepped to the side. “Mum’s in bed. Stay in the porch. I’ll need to be quick. Give me a moment to fetch the petty cash tin.”

As soon as Karen was out of sight, Constance jumped out of my bag and hissed, bushing out her fur as she snaked along the hall until she reached the lounge door.

As I moved forward, I got a massive dose of static and turned around. “Jeff, get your phone out. There’s paranormal activity here.” I rubbed my arms.

Constance scratched and hissed at the door until it opened.

“Come back here,” I said in a loud whisper as I followed her into the room.

Jeff came in behind us. It was dark inside the room, but with the light shining from the hall, I could see that Karen’s mother was still in her chair and not in bed as Karen had told us.

“She’s left her poor mum in the dark,” I whispered not wanting to wake her up.

Constance stood beside the chair, staring at Karen's mother from the side and gave a low meow with her hair bushed out.

My body fizzed with static. "There's something wrong," I said to Jeff as I pointed at the chair. "Get Constance."

Jeff passed me and bent to pick Constance up then looked directly at Karen's mother. "What the..."

"Get out of there." Karen gave a high-pitched cry from the door.

I jumped and held my chest, trying to catch my breath as the static intensified.

Jeff stared at Karen's mother, with his eyes wide open.

I would have been scared anyway, just from seeing his gaze but the fear was compounded as a female spirit rose from the chair.

"Tell Karen-May that I love her," she said. "But she needs to stop lying, to set herself free." She pointed directly at Karen who stood with the metal box full of the petty cash. Then the spirit disappeared.

Jeff held Constance in his arms as he pointed to the chair.

"Get out, now!" Karen shouted at us.

I ignored her wishes, closed my eyes and breathed in deeply while the static calmed down. I slowly reopened my eyes, it wouldn't have been the first time I'd seen a dead body. I needed to see it for myself and moved forward.

As I got there I jumped. Sitting in the rocking chair was a scarecrow, wearing a grey wig and presumably Karen's mother's clothes.

I swung around and pointed at the chair "Is this what Deloris found out? That you'd killed your mother?"

"Are you mad?" Karen said.

"You have a scarecrow in your lounge and are pretending it's your mother," Jeff said.

"And sitting it in front of the television," I said shaking my head. "And she's so forgiving."

"Who is?" Karen asked.

"Your mother, she just spoke to me."

Tears sprung into Karen's eyes. "You're lying."

"No, I'm not. She referred to you as Karen-May and said you have to stop lying to set yourself free." I paused. "And despite that, she said to me that she loves you."

Karen dropped to her knees and the petty cash fell to the floor with a clang.

I edged around the room and Jeff followed me with a struggling Constance in his arms. I wanted to get out of there, to call Brad.

As we passed Karen, hoping to escape she grabbed my legs. "I miss her so much," she cried. "She's dead."

"I gathered that," I said looking back at the scarecrow.

"We're going to have to call the police, Karen," Jeff said lifting his mobile.

Karen looked up with her eyes wide open. "What for?"

"So you can confess."

"It was years and years ago. We were all young."

"What you all killed your mother years ago?" I asked.

"No. I never killed Mother. She died a few months ago."

"What of?"

"Old age." She gestured across the room. "In that chair."

"But you killed Deloris," Jeff said.

"No, I did not."

"Look. Stand up," I said to Karen. "This isn't making sense."

"I'm confused," Jeff said,

"Of course, I didn't kill Mum." Karen stood up wiping her eyes, leaving the petty cash on the living room floor.

"So what's with the scarecrow?" Jeff pointed to the chair.

Karen sighed. "It's that lot. They always led me astray and got me into trouble. They said as soon as Mum died, they'd take me out on the town. Suzy said she would get me a make-over and knew a great aesthetician and hairdresser. Tracey said she wanted me to go in the pub every night and was going to introduce me to some men. Mark suggested we all go on a booze cruise. Fred said he'd take me out for dinner. But I just want to be left alone, so I pretended Mum was still alive." She puffed out and lifted her arms. "Is that such a crime?"

"And Deloris found out?"

Karen shook her head. "No. She never came to my house."

"How did no-one know your mother had died?" I asked.

"She didn't want a funeral, she was cremated and then I scattered her ashes over Cormorant Cove where she used to go bird watching with Dad."

"So what happened years ago?" Jeff asked.

"Pardon?"

"When I said your mum told you to stop lying and you needed to confess, you said it was years ago," I said, clarifying Jeff's question.

She wiped her eyes. "I need a tea to settle myself. I may as well tell you, come through to the kitchen."

Once seated Karen sighed. "We all stole the silver from the Church and sold it in Bristol. We had watched *The Italian Job* on television and hatched the plan as a gang. At the time, it had been an adventure. Years later, after Fred, Rosemary, Suzy and

Tracey returned from University, they got together with Mark and started the choir charity event to raise money to pay back the costs of the replacement. Part of the reason I stayed away was because I worried that we'd get found out. It's always eaten away at me, you see? They've been at the choir raising money ever since, to absolve their sins. But I've found it harder to live with the lie, knowing we broke the law."

"How did Deloris find out?" I asked.

"One of us must have told her. I don't know who."

"That's insane. So you all killed her," Jeff said with his eyes wide open. "Then all stuffed a mince pie into her mouth, one at a time?"

"Calm down, Jeff," I said. "There was only one mince pie in her mouth, not six."

"Oh yeah," he said in his seat and Constance jumped onto his lap, watching Karen closely.

Karen shook her head. "No one knows who did it. Everyone thinks it was one of the others. Mark and Tracey have been really off with me, so I'm guessing they think it was me. Fred is convinced it was Mark. Suzy is convinced it's Rosemary, as she hated her and had argued with her openly. But Suzy also said she doesn't care who it was, and that whoever did it deserves a medal. And if anyone found out, not tell the police, or you. So I've been thinking that it was Suzy that did it."

I glanced at my phone for the time. "Look, I think you should have a service for your Mum and do away with the scarecrow. I can get Lynn to do it for you."

Karen burst into tears again. "I feel so much better like a weight has been lifted from my shoulders." She stood up. "I'll just wash my face and then we'd better get up to the Church."

"What do you think, boss?" Jeff whispered as Karen went off to tidy herself up.

"I've no idea. And I can't think at the moment, we need to get this carol service done." I realised that whilst I had discovered a lot, I still had no clue who killed Deloris.

CHAPTER 10

Jeff, Karen, Constance and me, reached the Church, which was starting to fill up. Suzy rushed over to Jeff who groaned as she hung onto his arm.

"I need to warn you, Deloris' son is here." She pointed to a large man sitting at the front of the Church. "So we need to keep any negative talk of Deloris to a minimum." She pointed at me. "And no going around putting the idea in his head that she was murdered. No good will come of it."

I'd got to the stage where I didn't trust any of them. But one thing was for sure. I needed to speak to this man.

"Now come on, let's get to the vestry." She dragged Jeff off and Karen followed in silence.

I made a beeline for the first pew. “Hello, I’m Becky. Are you Deloris’ son?”

He stood up and I recognised the blue eyes. “I am indeed. I came to the service because Mother spoke of it constantly.” He smiled. “All she used to say was, I want to sing, I just want to sing.”

I felt a buzz of static fizzle up the back of my neck. They were the exact words I had been hearing from Deloris.

“I’m so sorry for your loss,” I said. “I hear your mother was at The Royal Academy of Music.”

He nodded. “And performed at The Royal Opera House. She sang like an angel.”

Hmmm, I thought. *Being tone deaf must run in the family.*

“Until she got ill, that is.”

“When was that?” I asked with a frown.

Constance poked her head out of my bag.

“In her thirties, just after she had given birth to me. She had been doing back-to-back shows while I was with my grandmother and had not taken care of her health. It took its toll. She ended up in hospital with pneumonia, which in turn affected her hearing and ultimately her singing. It left her slightly on the sharp side.”

It was more than slightly, but I made no comment. “So, she really did sing at the Royal Opera House?”

He nodded. "She was a single mother, too. It was frowned upon at the time, I was illegitimate but she always told me that my father was from the aristocracy. My father wanted his identify to remain a secret, and I respect that. I've had an extremely fortunate upbringing and am wealthy, thanks to him."

Wow, I thought. *Deloris' had the biggest secret of all.*

"Becky. Now."

I looked up to see Fred gesturing at me.

I turned back to Deloris' son. "I'm in the choir, I hope we do your mother proud."

My mind was swimming with information, my goal of investigating and wrapping this case up in one day, was making me giddy.

"Here she is," Lynn said beckoning me.

We stood in the vestry warming up as the church continued to fill. We wore our sparkly hats and Constance fitted in well with her sparkly collar.

I studied my fellow singers. At least I knew what the big secret was, that as teenagers they had been in a gang and stolen the silverware. Fred, was headmaster of the school now. It would not look good for his career if he was shown to have stolen from the church.

Karen, would also look bad at school. And as she had also taken money intended for the donkey sanctuary, she would not be trusted by anyone.

Mark would find it difficult for customers to let him into their houses and trust him if they discovered he was a thief.

Tracey's customers might find somewhere else to drink. And did her husband know? If he found out she had lied to him about the reason for starting the choir, he might think she was keeping other secrets from him, especially if Deloris had shown him the picture of her and Mark.

Then there was Suzy, although I wondered whether she would rather people thought she was a thief than find out she'd had plastic surgery.

And finally, Rosemary, who was high up in the W.I and a respected retired businesswoman. How would that affect her life if everyone knew she was a thief? On the other hand, she made no secret that she hated Deloris, even if she was the only one that had shed a tear, following her death. The only bad thing she had said about the woman was that she had bad fashion sense, mocking the dress she wore the day she died.

"Oh, no," I said out loud as I stared at Rosemary.

"What now?" The choir said collectively.

I put my hand to my mouth.

Fred put his hand up. "Whatever you have deduced, my girl, we don't want to know. We've a show to perform."

I ignored him. "It was you," I said pointing to

Rosemary. “You killed Deloris. You saw her after our practice, otherwise how could you have seen her snowman dress? She only got it just before our practice. It was you I saw in the hut with her at ten o’clock.”

“Really? You’re doing this now?” Suzy said throwing her arms in the air. “Carols by Candlelight is going to be ruined.”

“More like killer by candlelight,” Mark grumbled.

Rosemary burst into tears. “I told you it was all my fault.”

Lynn put an arm around her. “Let’s take five, lovey.”

“Five? The service begins in two minutes,” Fred said, his voice rising in pitch.

“I’ll never forgive myself,” Rosemary wailed.

“Shh,” Suzy said. “Please don’t open a can of worms.”

Lynn led Rosemary to a chair.

Karen watched on in silence, as if in shock.

‘I said so,” Suzy said with her arms crossed.

“This this isn’t a time for point scoring,” Tracey said. “But just leave Rosemary alone,” she said to me.

“You have no proof,” Suzy added.

“Er...” Jeff gestured at Rosemary. “I think she just confessed.”

"What happened?" I asked Rosemary in a soft voice as I crouched before her.

"Don't say anything without a lawyer," Mark said.

"You saw Deloris after the choir rehearsal, didn't you?" I said looking up at Rosemary. "Otherwise you would not have known she was wearing the Christmas snowman dress."

Rosemary nodded between sobs. "I was passing and heard her singing the solo. I went in to make peace with her and when I made a suggestion about cutting out one of the verses, she flew off the handle at me. She told me I was not allowed back in the choir, ever." She sniffed. "I was one of the founding members." She paused. "Then I was unkind. I told her she should watch her health and called her a pig."

"And?" I asked.

"And then she said she could eat what she liked and picked up a mince pie and stuffed the whole thing into her mouth."

"Then what?" Jeff asked.

"She stared at me. I stormed off then heard a crash. I thought she'd chucked a chair across the room or something. I didn't go back as I presumed whatever she had thrown, was meant to hit me."

"So how exactly did you kill her?" Jeff asked rubbing his scrappy beard.

"I went home. I should have gone and checked on her. She'd clearly fallen over and needed resuscitation and an ambulance."

I breathed out. "So, you never touched her?"

"It's all my fault," Rosemary wailed.

"So, you're telling me no-one killed Deloris?" Fred asked.

"She had a heart condition," I said.

"But why is she haunting you, boss?" Jeff asked.

Fred held his hand up. "We'll have to discuss this later. It's time for us to sing." He gestured at Rosemary. "Compose yourself, woman. We need to be professional."

THE FIRST THING I saw as we walked into the main church, were my parents. Mum with her straight brown hair and Dad with his red, longer than I remembered, curly hair. I gulped and felt tears spring to my eyes. I breathed in deeply. I knew I had to hold it together for the performance. Mum was soon wiping her eyes and Dad stared with his mouth wide open, gawping at Constance and then back at me. I smiled and waved at him. He obviously missed me. He looked totally stunned.

The carols went beautifully. It was so heartwarming to sing along with the congregation. As the programme ended, my hands fizzed. I looked up to see the spirit of a beautiful woman with ringlets in her hair. My mind was taken back to when I had climbed Deloris' staircase and seen the picture of the woman performing on stage.

Deloris? I thought.

She smiled at me as Constance hissed and her coat bushed out

Deloris moved towards me. *I want to sing.* I heard her say in my head.

She turned and stood in front of everyone.

I hurried over to the vicar and told him that I wanted to say a few words about Deloris.

He flared his nostrils at me, he wasn't my greatest fan. I'd hijacked one of his funerals back in the spring and my paranormal experiences, didn't exactly fit with his teachings. But still, he stepped back and nodded at me in agreement.

I just want to sing, Deloris said to me.

I stepped up to the pulpit, which was positioned to the right of the chorus.

"We wish for everyone to take a short silence, for us to remember those who will not be with us this Christmas," I said. "Especially remembering our missing choir member Deloris Noble." I nodded at her son who beamed at me and mouthed a thank you.

I closed my eyes.

As silence fell, Deloris' spirit began to sing *The First Noel.*

I opened my eyes, stunned and looked across to her. She stood at the front of the congregation in full voice. It was beautiful and my body filled with tingles, but not the static ghostly type, the sort I get when hearing beautiful music. Far from being sharp, she was perfectly in tune. I smiled as I watched on, mesmerised.

Constance sat down and was also quiet, although her fur remained bushed out.

I smiled as I looked around the congregation at everyone, so peaceful in their own thoughts. Some with their eyes closed, no doubt thinking of Deloris or their own lost loved ones. Then I stopped as my gaze rested on Dad. He stared directly at Deloris with his mouth agape.

As Deloris' spirit finished her song, Dad began to clap. I joined in and then the whole congregation gave applause, even though they clearly had not heard the beautiful performance. A door of light appeared in the church and I shielded my eyes as my heart was filled with love.

Dad squinted as he watched on.

The rest of the congregation chatted amongst themselves.

The vicar was praying.

I looked back at Deloris as she moved into the light. Then she was gone.

I raised my eyebrows and stared back at Dad. He exchanged a look with me, then glanced down at his hands. I knew he'd seen Deloris. And he knew I did too.

I shook my head. My father had some answering to do.

CHAPTER 11

The service was over and everyone had eaten the food which the parishioners had brought with them to share. Mum had monopolised me with her arm around my waist, as I watched Dad. He was looking incredibly stressed. Constance was acting strangely too, sticking to Jeff like glue and not coming anywhere near my parents.

I disentangled myself from Mum when a huge guy filled the church doorway – it was Brad.

I told Mum that I had to see someone and to meet me back at the house. I motioned for Brad to follow me to the vestry.

"So?" he asked once we were alone.

"It was natural causes."

"You sure?"

I nodded. "Brought on by an argument, but the

person she was arguing with did not touch her. Deloris was the one that stuffed the pie into her own mouth, in defiance, saying she could eat what she liked."

"That didn't turn out well."

"No. The person was rude to her, but not really something you go to jail for."

Brad let out a long breath. "Thank God."

"Yeah," I said realising it was heartfelt and not blasphemy. "And her spirit was only haunting me as she wanted to sing. But she moved on after the carol service."

"I probably should have accepted it was natural causes. My judgement was off. It's..."

"Fatherhood," I said with a smile.

"They've arrived. They did an emergency caesarean. Three girls all in working order."

I laughed at his use of description. "What are you doing here then? Go on." I gestured to the door.

He hesitated.

"You're going to make a great dad." I moved forward and hugged the bulk of his body. He stiffened and was so huge that my arms did not stretch the whole way around.

"I doubt that," he said.

I laughed and stepped backwards. "Trust me, I'm psychic."

He grunted and turned away.

"And Brad. Does this mean I can help again in future?"

"Don't push it, James," he said as he left. But I knew with complete certainty, he would call on my help again.

As Brad disappeared, Lynn came in. "What happened out there? I could feel a presence."

"Deloris sang beautifully, and then moved on. I spoke to her son earlier, she really was trained at The Royal Academy of Music. Her singing was affected by her becoming deaf through illness. But I'm a little concerned."

"Why?"

"I've seen two spirits today and neither were murdered."

"That'll be your gift developing."

I sighed. "There's no running away from it, is there, Lynn?"

"I'm afraid not." She gave me a hug and then stepped back. "Your parents went back with Jeff and Constance. I said I'd walk down with you as I'm parked at the hut."

"Talking about running away from a gift, did you know that my dad can see the dead?"

"Your Grandma never mentioned it to me. I knew her, but as I said, she kept herself to herself and was very private."

"He saw Deloris. He heard her sing."

"I wondered why he ended the silence by clapping."

"I can't believe he never told me about all of this. He never warned me. And there was me working myself up to explaining it to him, as he's always been so anti anything paranormal. And he knew all along!"

"Now don't get yourself worked up, lovey. It's Christmas Eve after all and you haven't seen him for two years."

I took a deep breath. "I know. I'll go easy on him."

I WENT into the house via the back door. Once inside the kitchen, Mum gave me another hug.

"It's so amazing to have you back," I said grinning from ear to ear. "Where's Dad?"

"He's in the snug. I'm a bit worried about him to be honest. He's probably tired. I'll go upstairs and change darling, then we can have a proper catch up."

I approached the snug and could hear Dad's voice through the closed door. "Mother. You need to leave."

Constance gave a long wailing meow.

I opened the door. "I see you're making friends with my cat."

He looked back at me, startled. "Becky." His hair

was practically standing on end, where presumably he had been running his hands through it. As I looked at Constance, I saw how similar their hair colour was.

I crossed my arms. "Does Mum know?"

Constance meowed and Dad glanced at her then back at me. He looked down and shook his head.

"Why didn't you tell me you could see the dead? And that I might be psychic too?"

"I didn't want you to grow up like I did. Having a freakish childhood."

Constance hissed at Dad and bushed out her fur. She seemed pretty angry.

I picked her up, worried that she would go for him. "Don't you like Dad, Connie?" I looked over at him. "I can't believe Grandma never told me. We were really close."

Constance gave a pitiful meow.

Dad ran a hand through his hair. "It was my fault. I made her promise not to mention it. Just in case you didn't develop the gift. I've spent a lifetime trying to get away from it. And to a certain extent it worked."

"But you can't ignore it in Branden Bay?"

He stared at my cat and shook his head slowly. "No."

Constance gave a satisfying meow.

"But don't tell your mother about you having this curse."

"Dad, the whole town knows." I laughed. "We have an awful lot of catching up to do."

ON CHRISTMAS MORNING, I woke up and stretched, feeling relaxed. There was no killer on the loose in Branden Bay. Deloris had moved on to the other side. I'd had an amazing night of peaceful sleep and Mum and Dad were home. I hadn't realised how on edge I'd felt, with them travelling the world and not knowing they were okay at any given moment. I felt as if a blanket of calm had covered my world. I breathed out and heard Constance meow and looked at the end of the bed. She was sitting next to a Christmas stocking.

I laughed. "What's this?"

I moved forward and saw a tag.

Things we collected on our trip. Merry Christmas darling, with love from Mum, Dad and Santa.

I smiled and decided to open it with them. I took it downstairs to find Mum in the kitchen.

"There you are, Becky. I've put the oven on. That turkey is huge," she said pointing to it on my worktop. "Maybe we should have put it on to cook, before we went to bed."

"Thanks Mum. And thanks for this." I lifted the stocking. "I have a gift for you as well. I wanted you to open it with Dad."

"Dad's in the shower, let's have a cuppa first. I've been a bit worried about him, he keeps calling your cat, Mother!"

I laughed. "Maybe I shouldn't have named her Constance after Grandma."

"She does have an uncanny resemblance to her, with her hair colour and eyes. Not to mention the way she sashays everywhere. You did have one special and glamorous granny. I'm so sorry we didn't make it back for the funeral."

"Mum, remember that Grandma would have hated you to interrupt your trip. She said to me before she passed that if she died while you were away, to tell you not to come back."

"I know. She was a loving lady."

Constance purred and jumped onto Mum's lap.

"And you're a loving cat," Mum said as she stroked her. "I think Dad is freaked out about this psychic stuff you told us about last night. And you being some sort of detective."

"I noticed."

"You know how Dad hates anything to do with the supernatural. I was surprised when he said he wanted to go to the church for the service last night," she said.

"Maybe I'll give you this present then, while he's out of the way." I handed Mum a wrapped scrap book in which I had put all of Izzy's articles about me in the local rag and the one from a national paper which had printed a story about me recovering a hoard of stolen diamonds. "I thought you would want to catch up on all I've been up to."

She flicked through the pages. "How amazing. I've no idea where you got this gift from."

"Grandma," I said.

"How odd that your father hates that sort of thing. It must have skipped a generation."

I gave a fluttery laugh. "Yes, I guess it did." Although I was not happy about continuing his lie, and I would be demanding that Dad told Mum at the earliest opportunity.

We spent a festive morning cutting up veg and making the side dishes, but Mum was right, the turkey was a monster of a bird and at twenty-six pounds, Christmas lunch was extremely delayed.

"I'm starving, darling," Dad said at five o'clock. "We'll have to take the legs off and cook them separately. The leg alone is enough for a family of six." He pulled the thermometer out of the breast. "It's still not to temperature."

Finally, two hours later it was ready.

"I'll turn the roasties up to brown." I was lucky to have two ovens.

Just as we were ready to sit down at the kitchen table, my bell rang.

"I wonder who this is?" I said, then opened my front door.

"Surprise!"

All my friends were standing outside.

"What are you lot doing here?" I asked.

"We wanted to surprise you," Annie said.

"Well, the surprise is, we're just about to eat a very late lunch," I said with a laugh.

They all filed in. Dannie, Izzy, Annie, Lynn, Jeff, H and his parents Carol and Paul.

"I don't believe this. The whole gang?"

"I picked Dannie up on the way back from London, sweetie," Izzy said.

"In an amazing limo," Dannie added with a hiccup. "We've had a few glasses of fizz on the way."

Izzy gave me a kiss on each cheek. "Neither of us could bare an entire Christmas Day with our respective families."

I gave Carol and Paul a hug.

H picked me up and whisked me into the empty cafe.

He lowered me down. "I got called back early as Brad has started his paternity leave. I've worked today, but up at Branden Bay Station, not the one in Exeter."

"You have to meet my parents."

"We'll eat it in here," I heard mum saying.

Dad followed her into the café, pushing the turkey on my hostess trolly. "There's enough for the whole town."

"The veggies and spuds might not stretch," I said with a laugh.

We were soon sitting at a long table in the café. I was surprised how the food actually spread out, considering it was meant for three. Mind you I always overdo it at Christmas. Seeing a table piled high with food was a bit of a tradition in our family and we often lived on the leftovers for a week. Dad had made up some extra gravy with H's help. I spied H chatting with Mum and Dad in the kitchen. I was so pleased they had finally met.

After everyone had eaten they helped themselves to the supply of cakes from the café display as dessert, Annie nudged H. "Go on."

"Your present." He handed me a small box. "If you accept it."

I stared at the little square box before me and my heart thud as everyone rapped on the table.

"Don't worry I checked with your parents first," H said with a grin.

I glanced at Dad who was looking a bit stunned.

Mum was smiling as she waved a glass of red wine in her hand.

I looked at H whose big brown eyes stared back at me, as if urging me to open the box.

I lifted the small lid and inside was a ring with a huge glinting diamond.

"Really?" I asked him with my eyebrows raised.

"Yes, really."

"Say yes," Dannie called out.

"Yes, yes, yes," everyone chanted.

I smiled at him. "Okay," I said slowly.

Everyone clapped and cheered as H whisked me out of the room.

In the hallway, H pushed the ring onto my finger.

I looked down. "This diamond is huge! You must have had some pay rise."

He winked at me. "I found the diamond on the pier."

I took a sharp intake of breath and held it for a couple of seconds. "No. You stole it?" I whispered. "From the haul of diamonds we recovered?"

"They were already stolen, I found it." He laughed and pulled me in close and I soon felt his lips on mine.

When he released me, I looked at the glinting ring on my finger. "Won't you get into trouble if someone you work with asks about it?"

"I told Brad as soon as I found the diamond. It

got caught in the tread of my shoe after we collected them up."

"What did he say?"

"He wasn't pleased. But said it would be too much hassle to report it. He didn't want internal investigations getting involved. He's got form with those guys. He gave me the number of a jeweller who used to be his informant and said no questions would be asked if I wanted it made up into a ring at some point."

"Really?"

"Yes. I think he's got a soft spot for you. And Becky, this engagement can be as long as we make it. There's no need for us to rush it. I just wanted you to know, I'm committed to our relationship and I want to be with your forever." His lips brushed against mine and then he kissed me so hard, I felt dizzy.

I smiled as he released me. "I want to be with you forever, too."

We returned to the café, to cheers from the people in my world who meant the most to me, I picked Constance up and she nuzzled my face.

I was so happy that I'd moved to Branden Bay.

I HOPE you enjoyed this series. It may not be the end, but it is the end of 'season one'. The characters really grew on me and I've really enjoyed writing these books. There may be a couple of questions you feel have been unanswered. This is because I've written these books in first person and there are some things Becky just won't ever find out! Although I have left clues in the books, to answer these questions, I have written a short story from the viewpoint of Alan, Becky's Dad which is FREE! If you want to read it, please visit www.kellymasonbooks.com or email me on kellymason@littleorchardpress.com

If you want to check out my historical series stepping back in time, one hundred years with the first of a traditional cozy mystery set in Millar's Hotel during the roaring twenties, look for it on your usual retailer.

If you would like to join my mailing list and receive a free digital copy of my novella about Becky's grandma Constance, then please visit www.kellymasonbooks.com

As ever, thanks for reading and for the encouragement I receive.

Kelly xx

ACKNOWLEDGMENTS

I'd like to thank my creative writing tutor Rosemary Dun, both inside the OU and out! You encouraged me to pursue novel writing and gave me so much information and guidance, I'm still reading the handouts! You are amazing. Thanks also goes to my brilliant mentors Alison Knight and Jenny Kane of Imagine Creative Writing and their Novel in a Year course, which gave me lots of help and kept me on track. And Alison is also my editor - thanks for all you do xx

Thanks to the inspirational friends I met through the Romantic Novelists' Association, and the Bristol writing community (I'm too scared to list everyone in case I miss someone off!) And to my Beta readers Cinnomen Matthews McGuigan, Michelle Armitage, Shell Rice Mortimer and Leanne Goodall. Thanks also to Helen Blenkinsop who is a guru on the 'hook' and amazon ads. And thanks to my best writing friends – Callie Hill, Claire O'Conner and Jenny

Treasure, for also being beta readers and for sharing the journey with me.

Thank you to my advance reader team who are really supportive and there for me, even from the first book. And especially Carol Kurimbokus who picks up those last pesky typos. I really appreciate it.

Thank you to those on my mailing list who interact with me. And thanks to those who send me cake ideas: Val, Keith, Carolyn, David, Janice, Tanith, Pamela-Anne, Nancy, Carrie-Ann, Carol, Sylvia, Marion, Christie and Betty.

Thanks to Tracey Hadfield who always has a ghost hunting story to scare me with.

Thanks to my sassy cats, even though they boss me about on a daily basis.

Thanks to my family for supporting me and reading my books, especially Dad, Uncle Stephen and Debjita.

And finally, thanks to Gary for putting up with me tapping away at the keyboard 24/7.

Printed in Dunstable, United Kingdom

67319882R00088